Traded Out

Samantha Wayland

Also by Samantha Wayland

Destiny Calls

With Grace

Fair Play (Hat Trick #1)

Two Man Advantage (Hat Trick #2)

End Game (Hat Trick #3)

Crashing the Net

Home & Away

Out of Her League

Checking It Twice

A Merry Little (Hat Trick) Christmas (Hat Trick #4)
Breaking Out

Traded Out

Dedication

For Aven Ellis, who has given me her friendship, her expertise, her sound advice, and hours and hours of laughs. Big thumbs-up to you, my friend.

Chapter One

Jamie Gallagher marched down the hallway toward the Edwardston Eagles' general manager's office, his head high and his expression bland. He attempted to radiate confidence, which was total bullshit because on the inside he was tied up in knots.

He could only imagine what his boss wanted to talk to him about now. Their last chat certainly hadn't been productive *or* pleasant.

Jamie was so busy trying to look bored that he was startled when Olle Svensson popped out of the locker room.

Olle stuttered to a stop and they eyed one another for a long moment.

"What?" Jamie asked, braced for anything.

He and Olle had just struck up a friendship when Jamie had made the monumentally terrible decision to hook up with some dude whose name he never learned, in a men's room of a bar he'd been certain no one he knew frequented, and been caught by most of the defensive corps—*including Olle*—when they'd come to take a piss.

It had been an interesting start to the season since then.

"Wilson wants to see me," Olle murmured, glancing away.

"Me, too," Jamie offered.

Olle nodded, silent, and started walking next to Jamie without looking at him again.

It was weird how a guy as massive as Olle could be so quiet, could take up so little room. At six and a half feet tall, with light blond hair to his shoulders and pale blue eyes, he should have been a *presence*. On the ice, Olle was a force to be reckoned with—an excellent defenseman who'd spent most of his season so far in the penalty box, much to the chagrin of their coaches. But off the ice, Olle was quiet and kept to himself.

He'd joined the Eagles a couple months ago at the start of

training camp, fresh off the plane from Sweden. Since then, he'd mostly looked like he regretted the decision, acting like he was ready to pull up stakes and bolt.

Jamie had thought it was weird at first. Now he could empathize. More and more, he'd been considering if it was time for him to leave Edwardston, and hockey, behind.

The hollow ache in his chest every time he thought about quitting hockey was the only reason he hadn't walked already. He wondered if this meeting would be what changed his mind. If it would send Olle scurrying back to Sweden.

Jamie took a deep breath and rapped his knuckles on Wilson's office door.

"Enter!"

Jamie hesitated and Olle finally looked at him. That piercing blue gaze felt like it could see right through Jamie and his bravado.

Steeling himself, Jamie threw open the door.

He'd been expecting the angry, ugly visage of his boss's face, but nothing else in the room made sense. For a second, he honestly wondered if he was dreaming.

He blinked, hard, but Chris Kimball, his friend from back home in Vancouver, was still standing there when Jamie opened his eyes again. And next to him was Rupert Smythe-Morrison, GM of the Moncton Ice Cats and one of Jamie's fucking *heroes*.

Rupert studied Jamie and Olle with his arms crossed over his chest. Jamie searched the room for some explanation, his eyes catching on a stack of papers on Wilson's desk.

Hope burst to life in Jamie's chest.

Except his asshole boss, Olle didn't know who any of the people in Wilson's office were, though the older guy in the fancy-looking suit was familiar for some reason.

Not from Edwardston, but...Olle was sure he'd seen him somewhere.

He'd definitely never seen the gorgeous blond grinning at

Jamie.

"Wilson," the suit guy said, "if you're satisfied the paperwork is complete, we should get going. We have a long drive and practice tomorrow morning."

Olle stared at the paperwork Wilson picked up and tapped into a tidy pile. "They're all yours."

Finally, Olle clued in.

Holy shit, they'd been traded.

The weirdest combination of relief and alarm swamped Olle. Something must have shown on his face, because the unknown man paused in the act of shoving papers into his briefcase.

He held out his hand to Olle.

Olle took it automatically.

"I'm Rupert Smythe-Morrison, GM of the Moncton Ice Cats. Welcome aboard."

"Please to meet you, Mr. Smythe-Morrison," Olle murmured.

"Just Rupert is fine."

Olle nodded, numb, and released Rupert's hand. Jamie shook it next, the first hint of a smile that Olle had seen on his face in weeks.

It took a few minutes for Rupert and Wilson to conduct a final, terse discussion. Wilson wasn't pretending he was anything other than relieved to see the back of Olle and Jamie. Rupert was managing not to sneer at him. Mostly.

Olle liked this Rupert guy already.

The thought had no more than settled in his mind when recognition struck. Rupert Smythe-Morrison, husband to Callum Smythe-Morrison, who'd quit the NHL to be with him. To be out. To raise a million kids or something.

The details were fuzzy, but Olle knew, at least, how he'd recognized Rupert's face. He'd pored over the article in *Hello Magazine* about their wedding, less interested in the cutesy pictures of the handsome couple and more interested in the fact that they owned and ran a hockey team.

Olle's hockey team, apparently.

Wilson shut the door behind them with a firm snap.

Dickhead.

Their little group paused, alone in the hallway.

Jamie turned to the gorgeous blond. "Chris?" Something squeezed in Olle's chest at the lost expression on Jamie's face. Like he couldn't believe what had happened.

Chris yanked Jamie into a tight hug. Jamie clung to him, his face buried in Chris's neck, and absolutely melted in his arms. Chris held on and didn't stagger when Jamie's full weight leaned into him, which was impressive because Jamie may have been one of the smallest guys in the league, but he was all sleek, heavy *muscle.*

Olle caught Rupert watching him. He quickly wiped the frown off his face and looked away, only to do a double take when he found Rupert's husband and another man walking toward them.

Callum Morrison had been one of the best goalies in the league for over a decade. Olle used to dream about playing with him when he was a kid. Come to that, Olle had dreamed about doing a lot of things with Callum when he was older, too.

So this was going to be awkward.

Not for the first time in the past few weeks, Olle seriously considered begging for his spot in the Swedish league back. Or maybe it was time to give up the dream altogether. Twenty-five wasn't too late to start university.

Chris finally took his hands off Jamie when *Callum fucking Morrison* and the other man, a good-looking guy with a shock of dark hair standing up on his head, joined them.

"Jamie," Chris said, a soft smile lighting up his face. "This is Tim. Tim, this is Jamie." Chris slid his hand into the dark-haired man's, their fingers weaving together.

Jamie grinned. Rupert and Callum looked on like a couple of proud parents.

Olle's mouth hung open.

Had he been traded, or had he gone down the fucking rabbit hole?

Chapter Two

Olle sat crammed in the back of the Smythe-Morrison minivan, his belongings packed in around him, barely leaving a view out the back window of Jamie following in his car with his hot friend Chris riding shotgun and Chris's equally hot boyfriend, Tim, in the backseat.

They were all smiling and laughing a lot.

They hadn't asked Olle to ride with them. Not that he was surprised, but he could have lived without being stuck in the family truckster with Dad and Dad, trying to stay off the grape jelly smeared across part of the seat.

Most guys got traded and they had to fly to wherever their new team was playing and jump right on the ice. Olle got traded and he got twenty minutes to pack up admittedly meager belongings at his apartment and a six hour drive with his new boss *and* his new boss's husband, who was unreasonably proud of his cherry-red minivan.

Olle decided it was time to buy a car once he got to Moncton, and quickly. Jamie used to drive him sometimes in Edwardston, but that was before that ill-timed trip to the men's room.

Fuck, he shouldn't be thinking about that.

"You okay back there?" Rupert asked.

"Did you do the trade to save Jamie?"

Rupert's eyebrows went up while Callum studied Olle in the rearview mirror. He tried not to squirm. He had no fucking idea why he'd asked. It was none of his business. And it wasn't like Rupert would tell him the truth. He probably had a canned media response ready to go.

"I did."

Olle blinked. So, no media response, then. "Oh. Well, sorry you got stuck with me in the process, I guess."

Rupert turned in his seat, facing Olle as much as he could

15

while wearing his seatbelt. "We're not *stuck* with you, Olle. You'll both fit perfectly where we had gaps."

There was the media response. "Right."

"You don't believe me."

Olle shrugged. "I know they wanted to get rid of me. I've had a rough stretch."

"You've had forty-eight penalty minutes in nine games," Callum said with a chuckle.

Olle looked down at his knees, cheeks hot, and shrugged again. He had no excuses, and it was horrifying that someone he grew up idolizing was calling him out on it.

"Which is actually *why* we asked for you along with Jamie," Rupert said.

Olle's eyes locked on his new, and apparently crazy, GM. "What?"

"We don't need a penalty box bench warmer, but I watched the games. All of them."

"I shouldn't have—"

"*Closely.*"

Olle stared at his hands in his lap, face burning.

"You were protecting him," Rupert said—and there wasn't any question in his voice. Olle's new GM was crazy and *astute*.

Olle glanced up but didn't say anything.

Rupert's gaze narrowed. "Did Jamie ever figure it out?"

"No." And that was how he wanted it.

"I figured as much," Rupert said with a nod, "given the suspicious looks he was shooting you."

"He doesn't trust me." *He shouldn't.*

"That's too bad. Maybe you could fix that by telling him the truth."

The truth? The truth was Olle was a lousy friend. He should have stayed and supported Jamie in the bar that night. Or in the locker room the next day. Or at any time other than on the ice.

Olle stared out the window. "What's to tell?"

"What's up with you and the gigantic hotty?" Tim asked from the backseat.

"That's Olle," Jamie said, keeping his voice even. "He's a nice guy."

"*Wow*. That was *really* convincing," Chris said. "If he's such a nice guy, why did you keep looking at him and frowning?"

Jamie sighed. "I just—I thought he was different. I thought we were friends."

"So, what happened?" Tim asked, leaning in.

Jamie focused on the road. He hadn't told Chris the details, just that he'd been outed and it wasn't going well. But Jamie trusted Chris, and Tim made Chris happy, so Jamie figured he trusted him by proxy, or something.

"Olle and a bunch of guys from the team caught me giving a guy head in the men's room at a bar," he said evenly.

"So?" Tim asked, as if this were something that happened every day.

Jamie decided then and there Chris had great taste in men.

He shrugged, his hands clenched white on the steering wheel. "So, he hasn't spoken to me since. Or looked at me," Jamie said shortly. And it hurt, damn it.

Tim flopped back into his seat. "Fuck. That sucks."

Chris frowned. "Wait, has he been an asshole about it?"

Jamie shrugged. "Not really, I guess? I don't know."

"Did he join in with the others in the locker room?" Chris asked, his eyes narrowing.

Jamie was grateful for Chris's protectiveness. "No. He just...sat and glared," he answered truthfully.

"At you?"

"At the wall, mostly."

"Huh," Tim said. "So he didn't say anything bad?"

"He didn't say *anything at all*. Until that night, I..."

Whatever was on his face made Chris's eyebrows go up and

Tim smirk.

"You never mentioned you had a *thing* for him," Chris said.

"It was...new? I don't know. We'd gotten to be friends and were hanging out. It wasn't a big thing. I never thought he would reciprocate or anything."

"Why not?" Tim asked.

"I don't know. He's hard to get a read on, I guess. He's a quiet guy. Shy."

"That's probably good since he's the size of a fucking house. And he's an absolute fucking *beast* on the ice."

"He is. But he's really gentle, too. And once he knows you a little, trusts you, he's got a lot to say. Or, he did."

Jamie missed that Olle. He'd been funny and sweet.

He'd also tucked Jamie in close with his arm over his shoulder while they'd watched a movie or a game the last couple times they'd hung out. It had cut through Jamie's loneliness and he'd leaned in, assuming it was a Swedish thing. Most of the world wasn't as uptight about men touching as North Americans were.

God knew what Olle thought of all that now.

"Wow," Chris said, watching Jamie. "You *really* had a thing for him."

"Yeah, well, it's a moot point now, right?" Jamie said, focusing on the road.

Welcome to Moncton.

The sign was the first things Olle saw as he was rousted from his nap by Rupert poking at his knee.

"You barely fit in this car," Rupert mused.

Olle sat up straighter and hunched his shoulders, pulling all his limbs in to take up less room.

"Please don't do that," Rupert said, watching him with a bewildered expression. "You can lounge all over the car if you want. I didn't mean to make you self-conscious."

Olle should be used to his own size by now, but sometimes he still felt weird about being too big for what most people considered normal spaces. He made every vehicle, even minivans, look like a clown car.

"Sorry?"

Rupert sighed. "Please don't apologize. We signed you in part because of your size. It's an asset and I'm sorry if I made you feel otherwise."

Olle blinked at Rupert. He was definitely a departure from any other hockey management Olle had experienced to date.

"Anyway," Rupert continued when Olle couldn't come up with anything intelligent to say, "I woke you up because we're almost home and you have a choice to make. I've gotten a text from Chris that Jamie will be staying with him and Tim while he gets settled."

Rupert watched him, waiting for some response.

"Okay?" Olle said.

"Right, so we can recommend a couple hotels, or you can come home with us."

Olle was sure he'd heard that wrong. "What?"

"You are welcome to stay with us. We have a guest suite, if you're worried you would have to share a bathroom with the kids. Though, honestly, they're tidier than this one," he said with a poke at his husband's arm.

Callum smirked. "Careful, dear husband, or I'll tell Olle all *your* bad habits."

Rupert was clearly not concerned, and shared a look with his husband that felt too intimate to witness.

"Okay. That would be nice. Thank you," Olle blurted, something in his chest loosening at the idea of not having to live alone, even if just for a little while. He almost regretted agreeing when Rupert's face lit up like a camp counselor meeting a fresh pack of campers.

"Wonderful. We'll head straight there to introduce you to the family and get some supper, then I can bring you to the rink tomorrow. Do you not drive at all?"

"No, I do. I need to get a car."

"We can help you with that," Callum said easily. "And you're welcome to stay as long as you wish, through to the end of the season if you'd like, but if you want to go apartment hunting, you can ask Alexei about it over dinner."

"Alexei...Belov? The goalie?"

"Yes, he's making dinner now, and it should be ready when we walk in the door."

Callum said it like it made sense, which it definitely didn't. Nor did the massive warehouse they drove directly *into* in order to park in a row of cars hidden inside. Or the insanely large and terrifyingly rickety elevator that took them up to the fourth floor.

By the time the doors opened to reveal a hallway better suited to the royal palace in Stockholm than an industrial building anywhere, Olle was revisiting his rabbit-hole theory.

A young boy stood waiting in the hallway. He stared up at Olle. "You've brought Thor round for supper, then?"

His accent was like Rupert's. And so was his face, for that matter. This had to be the younger brother Olle had read about.

Callum laughed and scooped the boy into his arms. "Oliver, this is Olle."

"It's nice to meet you," Oliver said politely. "I'm Oliver, but some people call me Ollie. It sounds like your name but it's not the same, is it?"

"No, it's not," Olle agreed with a smile. Mine is pronounced *Olle*. It's close."

Oliver cocked his head. "Like what people shout at a bullfight? *Olé!*"

Olle laughed. "It does sound a bit like that. I never thought of that."

Oliver grinned back, an instant bond formed over their names.

"Come in, come in," Rupert said with a wave, leading Olle into an apartment. It was warm and welcoming, with wood floors and thick, colorful rugs, big couches, and a brightly lit kitchen that gleamed with copper and granite. He couldn't even be surprised at this point. He was half-expecting the Queen of Hearts to join them for dinner. Or the Cheshire Cat to be curled up on his bed.

At the counter stood Alexei Belov, a man Olle knew well by reputation and because he couldn't get a fucking puck past him to save his damn life, and Mike Erdo, who was usually half the reason for that puck problem.

Olle waved like a complete dork. "Hey."

Mike waved back, equally dorky. Alexei rolled his eyes.

A teenager wandered into the room, carrying a baby.

"Ah. Perfect timing. This is Christian, and he's holding Eleanor," Rupert said. "Christian, this is Olle. He's going to stay here for a while."

Olle did more dork waves. Christian, slim and pale and better dressed than anyone else in the room—*probably not a hockey player, then*—went bright pink.

"Oh," he said quietly, blinking up at Olle. "Hi."

Christian couldn't seem to tear his eyes away.

"Well, then!" Callum said loudly, nudging Christian toward the couches. "How about I show Olle to his room?" He led the way down into the hallway just off the kitchen. Olle could see stairs going down at the end. "The family sleeps downstairs. If you need anything, don't hesitate to come get us. But you're in here," he said, pushing open a door on the right.

The bedroom was huge and beautiful, the bathroom nicer than any Olle had ever had. "Umm...okay. Thank you. This is really—"

Callum slung his arm around Olle's shoulder. Olle froze.

"Look, I don't know what the hell happened in Edwardston. I only heard the rumors. But none of that shit matters here. Respect me, and Rupert, our family, and our team, and you'll always be part of the Ice Cat organization, even if you end up on another team someday. That's how we run things around here.

That's how we run this family. We look out for one another. If you step out of line, you won't last long."

"That's not going to happen," Olle vowed.

"Good. Then it's a clean slate. Do something with it, eh?"

Chapter Three

Jamie paced in a hallway under the Moncton Arena and tried to shake his nerves. He'd had a great night hanging out with Tim and Chris at their place, but he'd woken up in a sweat an hour before his alarm and hadn't calmed down yet.

It was his first official day as an Ice Cat. Sure, the paperwork had been signed yesterday, but today they had practice. A new coach, a new team, a new locker room, and a new culture.

Tim and Chris had nothing but positive things to say, but they were trying to help him get settled, so it wasn't like they were going to lay the whole truth down on his first day.

He'd been dismayed when they'd insisted he drive himself in, coming up with a total bullshit reason why they had to take a separate car. Jamie had no idea what that was about, but it didn't bode well. He told himself it was cool if they needed some time alone now that Jamie was going to be around so much, and that it shouldn't sting at all.

He didn't recall Alexei Belov's legendary reputation as a prankster until he'd stepped through the door to the locker room and a gallon—or possibly ten—of cheap, foul-tasting lube dumped over his head.

There was a moment of ringing silence before everyone in the room burst into applause and laughter. Jamie cracked up, too, trying to shake the nasty shit from his hair and wipe it off his face. When he could see again, he found Tim and Chris standing well back, grinning. Even Olle, hovering by a locker with his name above it, chuckled. It was nice to see Olle's smile again but Jamie couldn't help but notice the conspicuous lack of lube all over Olle's head.

How did *he* get so lucky?

Not that Jamie was complaining. He was perfectly aware the league's rumor mill worked fast when it came to spreading juicy gossip, so at least *some* of these guys had to have heard what had happened in Edwardston.

But he had still gotten the same reception as everyone else on the team. He remembered, ten minutes too late, that Chris had been subjected to the same welcome. And he'd said most of the other guys had, too.

For the first time this season, Jamie felt *normal*—which wasn't something he thought he'd ever say while bathed in sexual lubricant.

Olle caught his gaze and grinned. Jamie smiled back for far too long, lost in how much he'd missed seeing this side of Olle, until Tim cleared his throat loudly from right beside Jamie. He jerked his eyes away and ignored Tim's delighted smirk.

Jamie's new coach came in, took one look at him, and rolled his eyes. "Gallagher, get your ass in the showers. You've got five minutes to get back to your locker to hear all the interesting shit I'm going to tell you. The rest of you, suit up now!"

Jamie met his deadline. Barely. He yanked on his base layers while Coach ran the team through the plan for practice, and didn't single out Jamie or Olle once. Jamie had just managed to pull his jersey on when the team stood to grab their remaining equipment and head out to the ice.

Olle planted his helmet on his head and was promptly lost in a huge cloud, a white, powdery substance bursting into the air or cascading down his hair and over his shoulders. For Olle's sake, Jamie hoped it was just flour and not itching powder.

The team howled, leaning on their lockers to steady themselves on their skates as they doubled up with laughter. Olle smirked good-naturedly, pulled off his helmet, and shook out his long hair. An even larger cloud of white dust filled the air and Jamie, along with everyone else, hobbled down the tunnel towards the ice at top speed, their coach leading the way and repeatedly muttering, "For fuck's sake, Belov."

Jamie couldn't remember when he'd last smiled so much, let alone while he was at work.

The next two days of practice were amazing. He hadn't played more than a game of shinny with Chris in years, but it was like they were back in school all over again. Like they hadn't stopped practicing passing and reading each other's moves on a daily basis. And Jamie was shocked to learn Tim would be centering them. Chris had told Jamie that management was cool they were dating, but it was more than that. They *supported* it. Hell, they took full *advantage* of it, since it translated to an almost preternatural connection on the ice.

And Jamie got to be a part of that. The reversal of fortunes was enough to give him whiplash.

He was practically *giddy* by the time he lined up for his first shift in a game as an Ice Cat. They were playing the Halifax Bears, the same team he'd played as an Eagle just last week. He knew a bunch of these guys were friends with some of the Eagles, but he wasn't expecting their right-wing to say, "You suck your way onto this team? I bet management loves those pretty lips of yours."

Jamie jerked upright, and the referee who had been about to drop the puck backed off and scowled at Jamie. Jamie cursed himself, not sure why *this* had shocked him. Apparently, it had only taken a few days in Moncton to make him soft.

Shoulders slumped, he bent to line up again, but before he could put his stick back on the ice, an Ice Cat jersey blew past him and slammed into the asshole who'd mouthed off.

Punches flew, most of them coming from Mike Erdo, Jamie's new teammate. A teammate who Jamie had spent maybe a total of two minutes speaking with since he'd arrived, and who couldn't possibly have heard what the asshole had said to Jamie.

Maybe there was bad blood between Mike and this guy already?

They went down on the ice in a tangle of limbs and landed with a thump. Jamie could hear the air wheeze out of the asshole's lungs when Mike landed on top of him.

Good.

Mike climbed to his feet, a big, satisfied grin on his slightly bloodied face.

"What was that about?" Jamie asked.

"That was notice," Mike said as he settled his shoulder pads and jersey back into place and made very direct eye contact with a few of the Bears within earshot.

"Of what?"

Mike pointed in the face of the Bears' captain and spat, "Zero tolerance of ignorant bullshit," before skating off to the penalty box like it was nothing.

Jamie looked around the ice, as if someone might explain to him what the hell had just happened.

He found Olle standing at his side, looking just as confused.

Olle could barely wrap his head around the kind of loyalty every single member of the Ice Cats displayed.

Olle knew Tim and Chris were in a relationship, and while they were seriously *not* subtle, they weren't out to the team. And he knew Alexei and Mike had been together for a long time, but they also had never made that known. Olle guessed most of the guys had no idea, and was honored to have been trusted.

But it wasn't just those guys wading into the fights and scuffles. Mike had gone first, but then it was *everyone*. Relentlessly. Like they'd been told it to do it. Like it was *the plan*. By the end of the game, there would be over a hundred minutes of penalties, no less than a dozen scuffles, and two more fights— all of which happened after someone gave Jamie a hard time.

During a stoppage in play, Olle looked up at the box where Rupert and Callum sat with their children. Oliver and Christian waved, and Olle waved back.

Did their dads do this?

To protect Jamie? To protect *him?*

Olle didn't think it was normal to feel such strong affection for his bosses. Especially not after just a few days.

But there it was.

While chaos reigned, Olle stuck close to Jamie in case someone tried to say or do anything while everyone's attention was elsewhere. He didn't drop his gloves, or try to wade into the fights, which was a nice fucking change, but he didn't let his guard down, either.

It didn't take long for Jamie to notice the pattern.

Somewhere between the seventh scuffle and third fight, Jamie turned his back on the excitement and lifted his eyebrows, silently asking Olle what the fuck he was doing there.

Olle watched Alexei try to trip someone who drifted too close to his net and pretended he didn't see the question on Jamie's face. When it was time to line up for puck drop again, Jamie was still there, watching him. He hoped he didn't image the little smile as he skated past.

The game ended with a solid win for the Ice Cats, and Olle with two assists. Having contributed, and accepting lots of pounding on his back and excited praise, was a nice change from the coach telling the room they'd won in spite of Olle's penalties. The team was jubilant as they stripped down, shoving and laughing as they moved between their lockers and the shower room. Towels were snapped, hung around necks, and occasionally tucked discreetly over hips, but almost no one seemed to notice or care who was naked and who wasn't.

The Eagles had practically showered fully clothed after Jamie had been outed, and Olle had taken to covering up, too, simply to avoid yet another annoying or offensive conversation. That was probably one of the many ways he'd let Jamie down.

Particularly since Olle didn't understand people's weirdness about nudity. More than one North American had accused him of being an exhibitionist, but Olle always shrugged it off.

It wasn't a kink. He was just Swedish.

Olle was pulling on his boxer briefs at his locker, grinning at the chirps and insults being slung around, when Rupert and Callum came into the room, smiling and laughing at the comments thrown their way.

Other than Jamie, these were the openly gay men in the Ice Cats organization. Olle looked around the room at the men in various states of undress, and noted the one or two guys who yanked their clothes on a little faster or hesitated to drop their towel, but most were utterly unfazed.

He also saw how Jamie watched the couple with ill-concealed hero worship. It was kind of adorable.

"Great game, guys!" Rupert called out, lifting his voice to be heard over the raucous room. He quickly had everyone's attention. "Just a reminder, the bus leaves tomorrow at three. Please be here by two-thirty. Also, as you've probably noted, we'll be on the road for Canadian Thanksgiving this week—*but*, we have the night off for American Thanksgiving."

"Fake Thanksgiving!" someone yelled.

Rupert rolled his eyes. "Right. So, the team will be providing a proper holiday meal on the road this week, and then, as has become our team tradition, you are all invited to our house to celebrate American Thanksgiving with our family."

A cheer went up. Olle was going to have to figure out what *any* of these Thanksgivings were about.

Rupert smiled and waved off the noise to finish up his announcements. As soon as he was done, Callum came straight to Olle's locker.

"We're going to invite Jamie, Tim, and Chris over for brunch tomorrow before the road trip. We want to check in with them. Make sure Jamie is doing okay."

"Okay. Great," Olle said, wondering how he could get out of being there. Not that he didn't want to be, but...

Callum watched him and waited. Olle wondered when he'd become so transparent.

"Jamie might..." Olle paused, hating what he was about to admit, "Jamie might be more comfortable if I'm not there. I can go out. Or stay in my room."

"What makes you say that?" Callum asked curiously.

"I...I don't know. Just a feeling, I guess."

"Would *you* feel more comfortable if you weren't there? Would you rather not spend time with Jamie?"

"What? *No.* That's not it at all," Olle said, rather too vehemently. "I like...I like Jamie." It was supposed to be a simple declaration of fact, but ended up sounding far more plaintive than he intended.

Callum arched an eyebrow. Olle could practically see the gears in his head spinning, and where this would normally be the point at which Olle would start deflecting like crazy, instead he just shrugged and said, quietly, "*A lot.* I like Jamie a lot."

Callum blinked, his surprise hidden as quickly as it had appeared. He smiled sympathetically. "Maybe that's a good reason to stay for brunch tomorrow, then. Who knows what could happen."

Olle nodded, but he *did* know what could happen—and that was *nothing*. Jamie had made it pretty clear that whatever had been growing between them before hadn't been what Olle thought. Hoped.

Callum squeezed Olle's arm, then went to Rupert's side to congratulate various players on their games and to chat with Coach. Olle trudged through his routine and out of the arena, the busy day catching up with him. He was grateful for Callum's arm around his shoulders as they made their way to the bright red minivan. He would never admit he was growing fond of the damn thing—and Callum's enthusiasm for it.

He was pretty fucking fond of the entire family, honestly. Christian had started talking to him like a normal person, though he still glowed a horrifying but adorable rosy pink at seemingly random intervals. Oliver was funny and way too smart for his own good. Even Mike and Alexei's constant teasing was starting to feel like home.

Olle passed out on his face the second he hit the pillow that night. He had barely moved by the time he woke up to the smell of bacon from the kitchen, and Alexei's voice booming out instructions to the children.

Then   the   doorbell   rang.

Chapter Four

Olle sprang out of bed, stumbling on his feet as he hastily made the bed and searched for his phone. He found it in yesterday's pants pocket and was dismayed to see it was already nine o'clock.

How the hell had he slept so late?

He'd wanted to shower again, but his post-game shower and some deodorant were going to have to hold him. Neither was doing much for his hair, though, which he hadn't taken the time to tie back before bed. It looked like something had nested on his head overnight. *Shit.*

He heard Jamie and his roommates being greeted at the door and hastily scraped his hair back into a messy bun that only served to further the impression that someone should check him for birds. Then he yanked on sweatpants, the cuffs of which clung to the middle of his calves—being super tall was a bitch—and a t-shirt.

He should be okay, though. Breakfast around here was often eaten in pajamas, including Callum and Rupert, who always looked rumpled and happy, and Mike and Alexei, who always looked so well-pressed it was obvious they didn't wear their pajamas to bed.

Olle stepped out of his room and learned the breakfast rules didn't apply to brunch.

Everyone was not only dressed, but Jamie, Tim, and Chris were wearing actual button-down shirts and dress slacks.

Of course they are, they're eating breakfast with their bosses.

Olle hovered in the hallway, about to execute an about-face, when Jamie spotted him.

Olle froze like a deer in headlights until Callum came up behind him and clapped him on the shoulder. Olle jumped and offered a weak smile. At least Callum was wearing jeans and sneakers, though Olle could do without the blatant sympathy in Callum's eyes as he glanced between Olle and Jamie.

Alexei finally took pity on him and demanded his assistance in the kitchen. Olle threw himself into helping and kept his head down, doing exactly what he was asked to do and ignoring the strange looks he was getting from Alexei and Mike.

Even Christian was looking at him oddly.

Maybe his hair was worse than he'd originally thought. Or maybe everyone was used to him being a lot more talkative. He'd definitely gotten over his shyness around here.

Olle brought dish after dish of food to the table, carefully skirting their guests so he wouldn't break up their conversations. He tried not to act weird, forcing himself to keep his shoulders back and his head up, but he still felt awkward and *too big*.

He was carrying what had to be ten pounds of breakfast potatoes to the table when Jamie struck up a conversation with Christian. Olle recognized the rosy glow in Christian's cheeks, his bright eyes locked on Jamie like a deer in headlights while Jamie asked him about his skating and school.

Olle's heart ached with sympathy as Christian's cheeks got redder. Man, Olle knew just how that felt. To have all of Jamie's attention on him, that big smile flashing, his hazel eyes bright, cheekbones high and fucking *perfect...*

Someone cleared their throat right behind Olle and he dropped the potatoes he'd been holding suspended an inch above the table with an ignominious thump. He refused to acknowledge Rupert's laughter and stomped back to the kitchen. He snatched the platter of bacon from Callum, who had clearly told his husband about Olle's confession, but at least had his back to the rest of the room when he grinned at Olle's scowl.

These people were the *worst* and Olle loved them for it.

Once all the food was on the table, they took their seats. Olle gritted his teeth at the blatant machinations of basically the entire family to ensure he ended up seated next to Jamie. They needn't have bothered, since all that did was make Olle want to be even quieter. Smaller.

Jamie was in his element. He had the whole table cracking up, first with stories from when he and Chris had been kids, and then by teasing Chris and Tim about their constant bickering because of Chris's messiness and Tim's obsessive cleanliness.

Olle listened and mostly kept his eyes on his plate.

"So, Jamie, how did you like your first game as an Ice Cat?" Callum asked.

"It was *great*," Jamie said. "Though I hope they don't all have that many penalties."

Callum laughed along with everyone else, but he kept one eye on Olle.

Olle suddenly wanted to dive under the table.

Callum smirked. "Well, someone had to give Olle the night off."

Olle wanted to die. He wanted to glare at Callum, the interfering pain in the ass, but instead stared at his plate. He could feel Jamie's eyes on him and wished fervently he had left his hair down to hide his face. Some of the guys were still laughing, and Olle hoped like hell they thought Callum was just teasing him about his penalties on the Eagles—and not working out why he'd taken them.

He barely registered the last ten minutes of the meal. As soon as Callum stood to clear the table, Olle shot to his feet to help.

Jamie rose more slowly. "Olle, can you show me your room?"

Olle didn't think he was imagining that the whole room came to a halt.

He blinked stupidly at Jamie as he left the table and walked toward the hallway. "It's this way, right? You looked like you rolled right out of bed when you came into the room this morning."

Olle winced, as did a few others at the table.

Rupert shot an accusatory glare at his husband, which Olle appreciated. Then Rupert opened his mouth to say something, god knew what, and Olle leaped into motion.

"Yeah, it's through that door," Olle said quickly, practically jogging to catch up with Jamie. "Go ahead in."

Jamie did.

Olle cast a glance back at the table and found everyone watching, then followed Jamie.

Jamie shut the door as soon as Olle stepped through it.

Olle shifted away nervously, looking around his own room like he'd never seen it before.

"What did Callum mean?" Jamie asked.

"About what?" Olle asked the far wall.

Jamie stepped closer, his chin tilted to see Olle's face, his voice firm. "Olle."

The prettiest, bluest eyes he'd ever seen zeroed in on him.

Jamie clenched his fists at his side, battling frustration and the urge to touch Olle equally. "What did Callum mean when he said the guys got in all those fights because you needed a night off?"

Olle looked away again and shrugged. "I don't know?"

Jamie took a deep breath, because that was bullshit, but he wasn't going to jump on Olle about it because he was still trying to rearrange things in his own mind. He'd spent a good chunk of breakfast running through their games with the Eagles. The fights and scuffles. The penalties Olle had taken. The time he'd tripped a teammate right after he'd refused to hug Jamie while celebrating a goal. The time Olle had crashed into their *own* goalie, pretending he'd lost control of his huge body, when Jamie knew how hard he worked to never let that happen.

Jamie thought he had it figured out, but he needed to be sure.

"Why don't you look at them?" *Why don't you look at* me?

Olle's eyes darted back to him. "What are you talking about?"

Jamie gestured toward the door. "Rupert. Callum. Everyone at that table."

"I look at them," Olle said, confused.

"You didn't. You didn't look at Christian when he was talking about his big figure skating tournament. Or at Alexei and Mike when they talked about their trip to New York last summer. You ignored them all."

"I didn't *ignore them*," Olle said vehemently. "I love this family. I would never do anything to hurt them." Olle stepped back. "Is that what you think of me?" he asked, taking another step, and another, gaining speed as he turned for the door. He'd almost got his hand around the knob when Jamie leaped forward and grabbed his arm.

"Then why wouldn't you look at them? Why won't you look at *me* anymore?"

Olle closed his eyes. "Because I'm embarrassed. Because they're meddling and I didn't know what to say. What to do." He paused, and Jamie thought he was done, but then he said, "I don't know how to apologize to you."

Something painful and sweet fluttered in Jamie's chest. "For what?"

"I was upset when I found you in that bathroom. I just...I shouldn't have run. I should have stayed and made sure you were okay."

"Why *did* you run?" Jamie asked.

"I thought we—I thought..." He shook his head, dismissing whatever he'd been about to say. "It doesn't matter. I should have handled it better. I'm sorry."

Jamie appreciated the apology, but the weeks that had followed had been *awful* and Olle had been part of that. He couldn't just let it go. "Why didn't you talk to me after? Why wouldn't you look at me?" Jamie was alarmed to feel the sting of tears in his eyes.

Olle stared at him, a helpless expression on his face. He opened his mouth a few times without managing any words before he screwed his eyes closed and whispered, "You broke my heart."

Jamie stopped breathing. "What?"

Olle shook his head. "I was an idiot. I thought we were...it doesn't matter. I should have been a better friend."

"You thought we were what?" Jamie asked.

"Dating," Olle admitted with a wince.

Jamie's fingers dug into tight muscles. "What? But we never—"

"I was nervous," Olle said in a rush. "I've never...not with a man. I thought maybe you hadn't either, so we were just...going slow." Olle's lips twisted bitterly. "Obviously, I was wrong."

Jamie slumped. Jesus fucking Christ, he was such an idiot. "God, I'm sorry."

"You don't have to apologize. I misunderstood."

"No, you didn't."

"You blowing that man in the bathroom says otherwise," Olle muttered, his gaze cutting to the side.

Jamie studied Olle's face. Ten minutes ago he would have thought this was disgust. God, he was such an asshole.

Olle wasn't disgusted. He was *hurt.*

Chapter Five

Olle didn't regret telling Jamie the truth, no matter how embarrassing it was, but *holy shit*, this was awkward. He could only hope this would make things better. Maybe he and Jamie could be friends again. Maybe Jamie wouldn't feel weird hanging out with a guy who'd admitted to an unrequited crush on him.

You broke my heart.

What on earth had made him say that?

"Do you remember what we'd done the night before?" Jamie asked.

Olle darted a look at Jamie, then away. "Yes."

"You put your arm around me, do you remember?"

While they'd been watching a movie. And Jamie had cuddled into his side.

Olle nodded.

"I thought you were just being nice. And Swedish. I thought you were *straight*," Jamie said, as if begging him to understand. "I thought nothing would ever happen, but your thumb rubbing over my arm and the smell of your shampoo, it got me all…"

Olle cocked his head, certain Jamie couldn't possibly mean—

"…*hot*," Jamie admitted. "I went out to hook up that next night. I thought if I could blow off some steam, we could keep doing that and it wouldn't slowly drive me insane, because I really, really liked it."

"You're very dumb."

Jamie accepted that with a helpless shrug.

"And not very observant."

"How was I supposed to know?" Jamie squawked.

"Do you see me cuddling anyone else on the team?" Olle asked, exasperated.

Jamie huffed. He was pouting and Olle despaired that he

found it adorable. He traced his fingertips over Jamie's pink cheeks. The skin was smooth over his cheekbones, then went rough with stubble along his jaw.

Jamie stared up at him, his lips parted, and didn't move.

Olle traced his fingers over the stubble again, fascinated.

"Olle?" Jamie asked, his voice soft.

Olle snatched his hand away.

"No!" Jamie said, grabbing Olle's wrist and bringing his hand back up. "Do it again."

Olle's cheeks burned and his heart beat hard against his ribs, but he did. Jamie hadn't shaved this morning, and while Olle would be the first to tease him about his sad playoff beard, he shivered to feel it under his fingertips.

Jamie's lower lip was caught between his teeth, and Olle couldn't resist touching there, too. Tugging on the thin skin and freeing it. He watched the blood rush back, turning it pink again.

Jamie pressed a palm to Olle's chest, right over his thumping heart. He lifted onto his toes and tipped his chin, his eyes darting to Olle's lips.

Jamie's fearlessness had always been what had drawn Olle. He bent slowly, the hair that had escaped the elastic hanging around his face, framing Jamie's as he got closer.

Their noses brushed and Jamie tilted his head to the side, surging up the last inch to press their lips together.

Olle caught Jamie instinctively, a hand spread across his back and another wrapped around his hip, holding him steady. Jamie kissed him again, and it was just as sweet.

A needy noise escaped Olle a second before someone pounded on the door right behind him and scared him half to death.

"Hey guys! If you're done with the tour, there's fresh coffee out here!" There was absolutely no reason for Callum to be shouting that loudly. He was also perfect aware that Olle drank *tea.*

Jamie and Olle stared at each other and listened to the not-so-innocent giggling coming through the door.

"We'll be right out!" Olle called, trying not to stare as Jamie shoved his hands into his jeans pockets and rearranged his dick.

Not that Olle was in better shape. The sweatpants had ended up being a bad idea for a lot of reasons.

With a deep breath, Olle opened the door and rolled his eyes when he found Callum standing right there, grinning at him like a lunatic. At least it was an effective erection killer.

"Did I hear something about fresh coffee?" Olle asked blandly.

"It's right here!" Alexei said helpfully, standing behind Callum and holding the pot aloft.

Jamie squeezed out of the room behind Olle, his hands fluttering over Olle's hips and waist. "I'd love some, please."

Chris took one look at him and his eyebrows shot up to his hairline.

Jamie ignored him and studiously doctored his coffee with his usual abundance of sugar. Olle felt like he was on stage, with all the attention he was getting, and wondered if this were a comedy or a tragedy.

He went back to his seat at the table, across from Christian. "I meant to ask you. Can I come watch you compete sometime?"

Christian smiled hesitantly. "You'd want to do that?"

"Sure. You watch us play hockey all the time, right?"

Christian laughed. "Yeah. Okay. I guess that would be cool."

Olle's phone buzzed in his pocket. He tugged it out while taking a sip of his lukewarm tea.

Go on a date with me?

It was a lucky thing he didn't spit his drink all over the table. It took him a solid thirty seconds of pretending to drink more before he could get his face back under control.

Then he sent his reply.

Yes.

Never in a million years did Jamie think it would be possible for the Moncton Ice Cats to be *too* nice and accepting, but within a day of leaving on their week-long road trip, it was very clear it would actually be an issue.

"Jamie! What about that guy?" David asked. He tilted his head toward the admittedly very handsome man at the hotel bar, who was doing a pretty good job pretending an entire hockey team wasn't staring at him.

"No," Jamie said with a laugh, tucking in closer to Olle, who'd planted himself in the corner of the booth. They'd checked into the hotel a couple hours ago and were supposed to be bonding as a team.

Jamie was now concerned what exactly that meant.

Olle didn't look at him, but he stretched his arm along the back of the banquette. It wasn't quite around Jamie, but he liked it.

"You haven't even looked at him," David protested.

Jamie rolled his eyes. "It's fine."

"No, it's not," David said firmly, capturing a number of their teammates' attention. "Look, I know you had a hard time with the Eagles, okay? But you don't have to live like a monk. If you want to go talk to him, and maybe go off and..."

Jamie almost laughed at David's vague hand waving, but his gut also curdled a little. "Sneak off to the men's room?" he asked, failing to keep the bitterness from his voice. He immediately regretted saying it. It wasn't like he had expected his reputation to magically repair itself overnight.

"No! I was going to say *get laid*," David said—*far* too loudly. He looked sincerely horrified. Or he did, until a slow grin spread across his face. "Though, you know what? Who cares? Maybe restrooms are your thing, and that's cool, too. If tiled walls and towel dispensers get you going, there's nothing wrong with that. Right, guys?"

Heads bobbed all around and Jamie couldn't help but laugh, his cheeks burning. Predictably, the conversation at the table immediately devolved into a series of lewd suggestions of what his teammates' various kinks might be.

Olle sank back into the corner, and while most of the table was captivated by Tim's insistence there *was* something hot about a quickie in the bathroom, Jamie slipped his hand beneath the table and squeezed Olle's knee. He didn't dare look at Olle's face, but smiled when Olle pressed their thighs together and kept them that way.

The team only got worse—or should he say, more enthusiastic?—after that.

By day three on the road, Jamie marched up to Rupert and suggested he change their name to the Moncton Matchmakers. Rupert guffawed, but his smile was proud, which did not help with Jamie's mounting exasperation.

Fortunately, the incessant meddling didn't prevent him from spending time with Olle, who derived far too much amusement from Jamie's torture. They sat together on the bus and on the bench at practice, and sometimes in the locker room. Jamie was certain the rest of the team didn't read anything into it, while being perfectly aware of the looks he was getting from Tim and Chris. And possibly Mike and Alexei.

Jamie liked being with Olle. Talking to him. Flirting with him. So much, in fact, that by the end of the week, he had no choice but to avoid being alone with him for fear of ruining the plan. He was determined to do this right. To go on a date with just the two of them.

Of course, it hadn't occurred to him there wouldn't be time to do that until they were home, which had *zero* bearing on how much he wanted to kiss Olle, *all the time.*

Jamie thought he was being subtle, since there was still so much time he could spend with Olle while the team was around, but it only took a day before Olle caught him in the hallway of their hotel and dragged him into the alcove with the ice machine.

"Did I do something wrong?"

Jamie's skin was buzzing, just from having Olle close. He clasped his hands behind his back to keep from *touching.*

"No," Jamie said, swaying closer.

"Then why are you avoiding me? Have you changed your mind?"

"*No.*" Jamie threw his good intentions out the window and stepped closer, pressing his palms to Olle's chest. "No, it's not that at all. Just the opposite. I can't..."

"You can't what?" Olle asked, sliding a hand onto Jamie's hip which resulted in the immediate scrambling of his brain.

"Oh, *fuck it*," Jamie muttered, dragging Olle's head closer and practically climbing him to press their lips together.

Olle let out a surprised grunt, but before Jamie could back off, let alone apologize, Olle was cupping a huge hand around the back of Jamie's head, another under Jamie's ass, and pulling him in close, his feet leaving the ground.

Jamie gasped and Olle's tongue slid into his mouth, enthusiastically tangling with Jamie's.

Was this going slow? Olle had said something about going slow, but damned if Jamie could remember now. He wrapped his legs around Olle's hips, a shameless and eager noise slipping out of his throat and killing any hope he'd had of retaining his dignity.

Who the fuck cared?

Olle clearly didn't. He turned and pressed Jamie to the wall, one hand cupping his head to protect it, the other digging into his ass.

Jamie was lost. Fucking *gone.* He sank his fingers into Olle's hair, clutching the long strands and tilting their heads so their noses bumped and their tongues and lips slid together. Olle tasted like chocolate and beer and sin and everything Jamie had ever wanted.

Olle leaned closer, grinding against Jamie's growing erection.

A door slamming down the hallway was like a gunshot in the tiny alcove. Olle stepped back and Jamie landed on his feet with a jarring thud, the wall behind him critical for keeping him upright.

Olle smiled at him while they listened to the footsteps

moving away down the hall.

"That's why," Jamie hissed in a whisper when he was sure no one would hear him.

Olle's smile got bigger. He pressed a palm to the wall by Jamie's ear and leaned in close. "Three more days?"

Jamie brushed their cheeks together. "What's in three days?"

"A night off, no team, no game. Our date."

Jamie's knees actually shook.

Chapter Six

Olle spent the next three days thinking about that kiss. It had been different than any kiss he'd had before and he'd liked everything about that. The stubble on Jamie's chin, his broad shoulders and strong legs, and how he weighed so much more than any woman Olle had been with. But even more than those things, he liked the eager noises Jamie had made, the way he'd climbed into Olle's arms. The way he'd fit there so perfectly.

By the time Jamie arrived at the door and politely asked a highly amused Callum if Olle was ready, Olle was jittery with anticipation. He threw a quick goodnight over his shoulder and ushered Jamie back into the hallway before anyone gave in to the urge to embarrass him. He could see it in their eyes.

Jamie leaned against the elevator wall and looked up at Olle through his lashes. "You look very nice."

Olle made a note to thank Rupert for talking him into this shirt. "Thank you. You do, too," Olle said.

He didn't want to be creepy, but he was having a hard time not staring. He didn't understand how he could ignore the dozens of naked asses he was exposed to literally every day, but would never get over Jamie's butt in well-tailored slacks.

Olle swallowed to moisten his dry mouth and trailed after Jamie out of the warehouse. Jamie seemed to have a plan, and Olle was happy to walk beside him regardless. In a few short blocks, they ducked into the House of Lau.

Olle smiled, delighted Jamie remembered his weakness for Chinese food.

The maître d' led them to a quiet booth in the back corner, surrounded by high banquettes and red velvet curtains to give them privacy. As soon as they slid in on opposite sides of the table, Jamie hooked his foot around Olle's ankle.

Olle couldn't control his grin. Or his dick, but that was hidden by the table, at least.

Jamie smiled back, and Olle realized this could end up being awkward, because he suddenly couldn't think of a thing to say. But, of course, at the heart of it, they'd started as friends, and they'd become friends again. There was plenty to talk about, and if they ever ran out, there was always hockey.

Halfway through their appetizers, and right around the time Olle admitted he hadn't dated anyone in a long while, he asked Jamie something he'd been wondering about. "When did you know?"

Jamie cocked his head. "That I'm gay?"

Olle nodded.

"I think I always knew," Jamie said with a shrug. "It just...*was.* I figured out pretty early it was something I was better off keeping to myself, though I ended up telling my parents when I was about fourteen. They weren't surprised. Worried, but not upset or anything."

Olle nodded. He didn't think his parents would be upset, either. No one seemed to care that his cousin was gay, and her girlfriend was the most popular member of the family on trivia night.

"You?" Jamie asked gently. "When did you know?"

"Um...about two hours after I met you?" Olle blurted, shrugging in the face of Jamie's stunned expression. "I mean, okay, I knew before that. I thought about it for a long time, but I didn't know what to do with it. You were the first who..."

"What?"

"Who I was attracted to and seemed to like me back? Or, at least, I thought so. And then..."

"You were right," Jamie said, touching Olle's hand. "You were definitely right."

Olle thought they must have looked like a couple of huge dorks, smiling at each other over their boneless spareribs.

They ended up spending two hours at the House of Lau, throwing their meal plans out the window and indulging in an embarrassing amount of flirting for two people who saw each other *all the time*. When the bill arrived, Jamie snatched it up.

"What?" Olle asked, still reaching for his wallet.

"Put it away, big guy," Jamie said. "I asked you on this date, so it's my treat."

Olle thought about that. "Okay, then would you like to go on a date with me?"

Jamie nodded, eyes sparkling. "Yes. When?"

Olle ran through their calendar in his head. "Thursday night?"

"Perfect."

Jamie led them outside and turned toward the warehouse. They stayed closer than was necessary on the sidewalk, their hands brushing until Jamie laced their fingers together in the elevator on the way up to Rupert and Callum's door.

"I had a nice night," Jamie said softly.

"I did, too."

Jamie stepped closer and slipped a hand around the back of Olle's neck.

Olle bent without hesitation, kissing Jamie gently. He was aware enough of the warehouse's security, and the extremely nosy natures of the residents, to wonder if they were on camera. It wasn't enough to stop him, though.

Jamie stepped away far too soon. "Good night."

"What?" Olle asked, his brain slow to catch up because of the kiss, and because it hadn't crossed his mind the night might be over. It wasn't even nine o'clock.

"I'll see you Thursday," Jamie said, pulling open the elevator doors and nudging Olle into the hallway.

"You'll see me tomorrow morning in the gym," Olle said, confused.

"That's different."

And it would be. But...

Jamie stayed on the elevator and Olle forced himself not to reach for him. To grab him and haul him close.

"Where are you going?" Olle asked, bewildered.

"Home."

"But..."

Jamie hit the button to go back down. "We're going slow, remember?"

Olle's mouth dropped open, but before he could say anything, Jamie was gone.

Their date on Thursday went even better than the first. At least, Jamie thought so as he drove back to Tim and Chris's place afterwards, picturing Olle's face when Jamie had walked away. They'd kissed longer this time. Long enough for his tongue to slip into Olle's mouth and twist with his. Long enough for Olle to drag him closer and slide a thigh between Jamie's.

Unfortunately, the next date wouldn't be for another week and by the end of the night they were both almost nodding off into their desserts and the waiter was sending them concerned looks.

When Jamie had suggested taking it slow, he hadn't given enough consideration to their schedule. They were on the road more often than not, and that meant meals with the team, and drinks with the team, and bonding with the team, and...well, their team was great. And they clearly wanted Jamie and Olle to feel welcome. And Jamie was grateful, but honest to fucking god, by the time all the team activities were done, not to mention the actual hockey, he was lucky to finish jerking off before he passed out.

Hockey was fucking hard work. Hockey and incessant travel was *exhausting*.

And his dick was starting to chafe.

He and Olle grabbed quiet moments when they could, and those were amazing. Maybe linking their fingers for thirty seconds when they were alone in the elevator wasn't much, but it meant something. And at least once per road trip, they made a point of waving off the team's attempts at dragging them out somewhere so they could curl up together and watch a movie, or just talk. They reviewed game tape together, hit the gym at the same times, and managed to eat out alone on a few occasions.

For their fourth date, Olle had invited Jamie over for Movie Night at Callum and Rupert's house, which was, apparently, a *big deal*. It was a command performance for the entire family, which included Alexei and Mike—who were *definitely* together, but, like Tim and Chris, not out to the whole team.

Though, honestly, Tim would have to take lessons in subtlety before the team couldn't *guess*.

Movie night was fun from the moment he'd arrived to find Olle racing through the living room with Oliver on his back, pointing over Olle's shoulder at his brother and bellowing about charging the line. Dinner was delicious and involved a near-constant barrage of affectionate insults and teasing. And Jamie wasn't very embarrassed to cry at Frozen, along with at least half the other adults present.

Olle held his hand under the blankets, and Jamie felt stupidly happy—and achingly aware of Olle's bedroom, just a few feet away.

This was another issue Jamie had not given enough consideration when he'd embarked on the whole going-slow thing. He lived in Chris and Tim's guest room, just one thin—*so fucking thin*—wall away from their bedroom. Which was the same situation they'd found themselves in at countless hotels, surrounded by their teammates, often with connecting doors that were habitually left open. And Olle lived in the middle of Grand Central Station, for fuck's sake, surrounded by children—who at least could be trusted to be discreet, unlike the rest of the household, who were bound to tease them for all eternity.

Jamie shuddered just thinking about it. Then he shuddered again, because he was fucking horny, and it would be worth embarrassing the hell out of himself if it meant he could get some relief and finally, *finally* be with Olle.

There had been kissing over the last couple weeks. *A lot* of kissing. And Jamie had made a study of every inch of Olle's skin from the waist up. From Olle's sharp collarbones to his sensitive nipples and ticklish flanks. Jamie hadn't realized he'd be into being so much smaller than his partner, but god fucking help him, he was *so* into it.

Olle was always gentle, learning Jamie as carefully as Jamie was learning him. Recently, they'd spent the precious little time they could steal pressed close, their hips moving against one another, their hearts pounding. Olle's hands shook sometimes, his hips stuttering as helplessly as Jamie's, and Jamie thought they'd both die if they didn't move things along soon. He was sure Olle felt the same way, given his long, frustrated groans when they were interrupted or ran out of time.

When date number...shit—Seven? Eight? There'd officially been enough of them that Jamie was losing track, which was awesome—finally happened, Jamie was hoping they'd manage at least a little alone time, even if he had to further his reputation as a man who liked bathrooms too much. He was bouncing up and down on his toes in the elevator, eager to grab Olle and maybe hit the House of Lau for an early-ish supper, then...hell, he'd ravish Olle in a fucking alley on the way home if he had to.

He lifted a hand, but the door flew open before he could knock.

"Oh, thank god, you're early," Olle said, breathless.

He looked disheveled, his hair wild, like he'd been running his hands through it. He glanced up and down the hallway, clenched his fist in Jamie's t-shirt, and hauled him through the door.

A frisson of fear went down Jamie's back, then Olle's mouth was on his and Jamie no longer cared if there was any danger. The building could burn down around them. Be stormed by commandos. He was good.

Olle wasn't messing around, either. His hands cupped Jamie's face as he kicked the door shut and pressed Jamie against the cold wood. His tongue plunged between Jamie's lips.

Jamie was definitely *definitely* better than good.

When Olle tore his mouth away to press biting kisses along Jamie's cheek and jaw, Jamie tilted his head, trying to help *and* regain his sanity. "Where is everyone?" he gasped.

"Out," Olle growled into his neck. "For at least two hours. Maybe more."

Jamie shoved Olle away. "What?"

Olle was panting. "They're out. For dinner and a movie."

"We're *alone*?" Jamie asked, hardly able to believe it.

Olle nodded slowly, studying Jamie's face. "Is that okay?"

"Is that okay?" Jamie repeated. "*Is that okay? Are you kidding*?"

Olle laughed and grabbed Jamie's hand, striding toward his room with Jamie in his wake. Jamie practically fell over his own feet in his eagerness to keep up.

As soon as the door shut behind them, Olle towed Jamie in and Jamie lifted onto his toes, his chin tipped in anticipation. He didn't expect Olle's hands to curl around his hips and cup his ass before lifting him right off the ground.

Jamie wound his arms and legs around Olle, and lost himself in Olle's drugging kisses. Olle shifted Jamie closer, lower, until Olle's erection pressed to Jamie's and he could barely *breathe,* let alone kiss.

Chapter Seven

Olle kept reminding himself they were supposed to be going slow. That was what Jamie wanted. Though Olle was pretty sure that was because Jamie thought it was what Olle needed.

And Olle needed anything *but.*

He held Jamie close, kissed him deeply, and it wasn't enough. He didn't know if anything would ever be enough, if he'd ever get his fill of Jamie, but he wanted to find out.

Like, *now.*

He took three big steps across the room and tossed Jamie onto the bed, thoroughly enjoying the shock on Jamie's face. The way his gaze went hot and his cheeks pink. Olle yanked Jamie's shoes off and Jamie sat up.

Olle paused. "Is this okay?"

Jamie tore his shirt off, tossing it across the room. "Does that answer your question?"

Olle grinned and threw his own shirt in the same direction, then reached for the button on his jeans. He bit his lip, hesitating.

"Please," Jamie said hoarsely. "If you're okay with it, I'm okay with it. And I don't just mean your pants, though please, god, I will be so fucking happy if you take off your pants. But I'm also okay with anything you want to do. And whatever you don't want to do. That's okay, too."

Olle had to swallow twice to make his voice work. "I want to do it all."

The flush worked its way down Jamie's chest. "Okay." He watched avidly as Olle pushed his jeans down and stepped out of them.

Of course, Jamie had seen him do this hundreds of times before, but context was everything. The erection tenting Olle's boxer briefs was not part of the deal in the locker room.

Nor was the ache of vulnerability, of feeling exposed.

"Now you?" he asked.

Jamie scrambled to shuck his pants, ending up on his knees, crawling across the bed to Olle. He skimmed his hands down Olle's chest and belly. "I have to be honest," Jamie said, his eyes following his own touch, his voice serious. "I'm not going to last five minutes."

At first Olle thought he'd misheard, but Jamie appeared utterly sincere and chagrined. Olle burst into laughter, his heart aching in his chest.

Jamie shrugged. "I thought I should warn you."

Olle cupped Jamie's face in his hands. "You make everything easy," Olle said, the words tumbling out of his mouth.

"What do you mean?" Jamie asked, his head cocked to the side.

Olle ran his fingers though Jamie's hair, his other thumb tracing Jamie's cheekbone—a habit he'd indulged in more and more as the weeks had passed. Olle couldn't believe someone as beautiful as Jamie wanted to kiss him. That someone as funny and bright as Jamie wanted to *be* with someone as big and shy as Olle. "I just mean you make me laugh. You make me...*happy*."

For a second, Jamie looked like he couldn't decide if he was going to laugh or cry. Then he crushed his mouth to Olle's, this kiss different than all the ones before—slow and sweet and like Jamie was trying to tell him something.

Like maybe Olle made Jamie happy, too.

Olle climbed up on the bed, moving them to the middle of the mattress and lowering Jamie onto his back, his mouth never leaving Jamie's.

Jamie's thighs hugged his flanks, his hands tugging Olle closer when he held some of his weight off. Jamie wasn't having it. He dug his heels into Olle's ass and drew him in, moaning when Olle smashed him into the mattress.

Jamie's cock dug into Olle's belly and Olle wanted to feel more. He wanted to do something about it. He hitched himself up Jamie's body, curling his back to keep kissing and bring their hips together. His cock rubbed along Jamie's, separated only by two thin layers of cotton, and he shuddered. Jesus Christ, that was good. He rolled his hips again and Jamie keened into his mouth.

Jamie's hands were everywhere, smoothing up Olle's back and carding through his hair, pulling him closer and holding tight. Olle worked their hips together, gasping into their kiss when Jamie thrust up against him.

Yeah, Olle wasn't going to last any longer than Jamie.

He'd known what he wanted from the moment Jamie had slid into the seat across from him at lunch during their first team outing in Edwardston. His heart had skipped a beat, and he'd smiled back at Jamie, helpless against his quick humor.

Jamie's hands rubbed up Olle's ribs, curling under to cup his pecs and smooth back down the center of his belly. Jamie's finger dipped into Olle's bellybutton and his breath caught.

He lifted his head, mesmerized by how debauched Jamie looked, his lips swollen and cheeks flushed as he traced his fingertips through the line of hair that disappeared below the elastic of Olle's boxers. His cock jerked, trying to leap into Jamie's hand as his fingers slipped lower, beneath elastic and cotton.

Arms trembling, Olle whimpered.

Jamie curled his hand around Olle's cock and Olle's heart stopped before taking off at a gallop, pounding in his ears. Jamie's grip was strong, rough with callouses. There was no hesitation. No uncertainty.

Pleasure curled Olle's spine, his thighs and belly going tight. He closed his eyes and tried to suck air into his lungs. For some damn reason, Jamie's highlight reel played behind his eyelids.

"What are you thinking about?" Jamie whispered.

"Hockey."

Jamie's hand stopped its slow drag up Olle's shaft. "What?"

Olle grimaced, trying to figure out how the hell he was going to explain this. "Your hands are so *soft* on the ice, with the puck. It's gorgeous. I watch you and it..."

"Turns you on?" Jamie asked skeptically.

Olle opened his eyes to see Jamie appeared absolutely *delighted* by the idea. He was never going to let Olle live this down.

Olle was okay with that. "Yes."

Jamie laughed, a big, joyous sound that stole what little breath Olle had left. Jamie wriggled beneath him, shoving down his own underwear, and using his hands and then his feet to push Olle's away, too. The moment his cock popped free, it bumped into Jamie's, the sensitive head smearing moisture over the soft skin of Jamie's belly. Olle couldn't think, couldn't focus on anything but what that felt like, trying to memorize it.

His brain jolted back online when Jamie rolled them to the side and climbed on top of him. Jamie kissed him once, hard, then was gone, sliding his body between Olle's legs, his chest rubbing over Olle's aching cock and his perfect butt lifting into the air, perched above the long trench of his spine. His wicked grin was the only warning before he took the tip of Olle's cock into his mouth.

"*Oh fuck*!" Olle bellowed.

Jamie's eyes widened, and it was obvious he was laughing, but he didn't stop *sucking.* Olle squirmed as Jamie slid his tongue over the tip of Olle's cock, making slow circles as he began to bob his head, little dips that rubbed his soft, wet, warm lips along Olle's shaft and sent shocks of pleasure firing through his body.

Olle came unmoored, his body beyond his control and his orgasm rushing up on him. He patted Jamie's hair, trying to push him back as he croaked, "Jamie. You have to stop or I'm going to…

Jamie hummed happily and sucked Olle in farther.

Olle whited out, his orgasm exploding from deep inside and roaring out his cock into Jamie's beautiful mouth. Olle's eyes rolled back in his head, his brain drunk on endorphins, his body thrashing against the bed.

Jamie let Olle's cock slip from between his lips. "Oh god, I have to…I'm just going to…" he gasped as he crawled up Olle's body.

Olle snapped out of his stupor and curled his hands about Jamie's hips, unsure what he should do until Jamie sat on his stomach and grabbed his own cock in a punishing grip, jerking himself fast and hard.

Olle batted his arm away without thinking, wrapping his hand instead around Jamie's cock. The shaft was rigid and lined with veins that pressed into Olle's palm, the head red and shiny. He rubbed his thumb over it, spreading the pre-come around before dragging his fist back down.

This was the first time Olle had touched a cock that wasn't his own, and it struck him how much it made *sense*. None of that confusing clitoris shit to deal with. Olle knew ten things to try, right off the bat, easily judging his success by the twitch of Jamie's hips and the expression on his face.

Jamie's mouth hung open, his head limp on his neck as he stared down at Olle's hand moving over him. Olle cupped Jamie's balls in his other hand, a thrill rushing through him when he felt how hard they were. How tight.

He loved that he'd made Jamie feel this way. That he'd reduced this dazzling, graceful man into a panting mess.

"I want you to come all over me," Olle said, moving his hand faster.

Jamie's eyes slammed shut and dug his fingers into Olle's ribs as he keened and did exactly as Olle asked, striping his belly with warm come. Olle watched, mesmerized by how Jamie's thighs trembled and his belly jerked.

Olle encouraged each powerful pulse with his hands, and felt an answering tug in his gut.

He couldn't wait to do it again.

Chapter Eight

"Jamie! I have the perfect guy for you," Bryan announced as he sat down across the table.

Jamie continued to chew his pizza and absolutely did not roll his eyes.

"I'm good, thanks," Jamie said once he'd swallowed the bite.

They were at a good Italian place in Sydney on Cape Breton, and Jamie was enjoying his slice of pie, his nice cold beer, and the warmth of Olle pressed along his side in the undersized booth.

The team had taken to dragging a bunch of tables together, often with a booth, and packing themselves into as little space as possible. Jamie had never appreciated hockey players' lack of personal space boundaries more, since Olle always liked the corner, and that meant Jamie had a perfectly innocent reason to be practically in Olle's lap most of the time.

They still called these team bonding dinners, but more and more, it was about two-thirds of the team jammed together, including Jamie and Olle and their friends, and about one-third who sat at the other end of the table, or ducked out early, or sometimes didn't come along at all.

No one, including Rupert, seemed concerned about that, so Jamie wasn't either. It probably wasn't a coincidence these were the same guys who often dressed and undressed where Jamie couldn't see them.

"But he's my cousin," Bryan said, rubbing his hands together with enthusiasm. "Super nice guy, I've known him my whole life and can totally vouch for him."

Before Jamie could decline politely again, Olle put his elbows on the table and leaned forward. "What makes you think he's perfect for Jamie?"

Bryan blinked owlishly.

Jamie choked back his laughter. It was hard to tell if Bryan was more surprised that Olle had spoken up, since he was usually content to sit back and listen, or if the deer-in-headlights look was because now he had to come up with an answer besides "he's gay".

Bryan finally arrived at, "He's really nice."

Olle nodded. "And Jamie is really nice, too, right?"

"Yeah?"

"What else?"

Bryan shrugged. "I don't know, man. He's a good guy."

"Good looking?"

Bryan blinked. "He's my cousin."

Jamie felt Olle tremble with silent laughter but nothing showed on his face.

"Does he play hockey?" Olle asked.

"No?" Bryan said, sounding confused.

"What does he do?"

Bryan shrugged. "Something to do with fashion, I think?"

Mike guffawed a few seats down the table. Jamie shoved a huge bite of pizza into his mouth.

"Fashion," Olle repeated as if fascinated. "And where does he do fashion?"

"Uh...Montreal?" Bryan said.

Olle nodded again, as if this made sense. "So, only a ten-hour drive. What are his other interests?"

"He...ahh..." Bryan was clearly at a loss. Jamie almost felt sorry for him. "He has cats?"

Almost.

Now Alexei was giggling uncontrollably, too. Half the team watched him with varying degrees of alarm because goalies could be unpredictable.

"Jamie is allergic to cats," Olle said flatly.

"Oh."

"Bryan," Olle continued, "does your cousin have anything in

common with Jamie other than being gay?"

"Ummm…"

"Because, I don't know if you know this, but just because two people are gay, it doesn't mean they're automatically compatible," Olle said in the same voice a teacher would use with a small child who was going to have their world view blown apart.

Half the table was listening in, now, and a good portion of them were laughing too hard to eat.

"But…" Bryan started.

Jamie took pity. "It's cool, Bry. I'm not mad and I appreciate you're trying to do a nice thing, but Olle is right. It doesn't sound like your cousin and I have a lot in common."

"I guess not," Bryan said, slumping. "I just…"

"What?" Jamie asked, curious.

"It doesn't seem fair. The team always goes to places where most of us who want to can meet someone, and you don't get that chance."

Which was both really sweet and probably not entirely true. But either way, Jamie was touched Bryan cared at all, and that a bunch of the guys around Bryan were nodding their heads.

Jamie very carefully did not look at Olle. "I'm okay, though. I promise."

"*I know*," David said, as if a grand idea had struck him. Jamie was filled with dread. "We could go to a gay bar some night."

Alexei's beer came out his nose. Mike buried his face in his hands, laughing so hard he'd gone silent. Tim and Chris grinned like lunatics, while everyone else around them appeared to be varying levels of terrified.

But god love this fucking team, most of them were still nodding.

"There must be some of those bars in the cities we visit, right?" Dave continued, blissfully unaware of the reactions around him. "Bryan, maybe your cousin knows."

"That's really not necessary, guys," Jamie said. "Really, I have a—"

"You have a what!?" David asked, leaning in. "Do you have a boyfriend?"

"I was going to say a full plate," Jamie said blandly.

"Then why are you blushing?" Bryan asked.

"No reason. I mean, except how you all want to discuss my love life."

"So, you're admitting you *have* a love life?" Tim asked, flinching when Chris kicked him under the table.

Olle smirked and lifted one eyebrow. Jamie didn't know what to make of that look, but it wasn't, "Don't you dare say a word" or "I'm freaking out here". Olle, clearly, wasn't about to say anything, and Jamie wasn't going to out him, of course. But maybe he could get the guys to lay off with the constant attempts at matchmaking.

"So what if I do?" Jamie asked, feeling reckless.

A collective howl went up from the table, everyone ignoring Jamie's flapping hands and requests to keep it down. They were going to make a scene, which was *not* what Jamie needed or wanted. It was one thing to be out to the team, and maybe even most of the league, but if anyone had leaked it to the press, the press wasn't printing it, leaving the public blissfully unaware. Jamie would like to keep it that way.

He snuck a look at Olle and was delighted to see he was laughing at everyone's reaction, appearing entirely unconcerned. Olle's trust warmed him.

"The guy in the bathroom?" Dave asked.

"What? No! Not him," Jamie said laughing. God, he didn't even know that guy's name, which wasn't something he was going to admit aloud.

Jamie didn't realize his mistake until he saw the calculating expressions on several of his teammate's faces. *Shit.* He'd more or less confirmed a boyfriend did exist, and then either confessed to cheating on him, having an open relationship, or having taken up with someone since the bathroom incident.

His instinct was to clarify. He didn't like the idea someone might think he was a cheater, but he didn't want to go down the rabbit hole of questions that would follow. He didn't have a doubt in his mind that his friends would hoard every clue he gave them and try to ferret out the truth.

"So, who is he?" Bryan asked. "Can we meet him?"

"He's not out," he said firmly, mentally preparing a lecture for his well-meaning and clueless teammates.

An unnecessary exercise, since they all accepted that without hesitation.

"Cool," Bryan said. "We respect that."

Jamie wondered if Tim and Chris noticed everyone studiously not looking at them.

Olle loved this team and the friends he—and Jamie—had made on it.

They were usually ridiculous, and sometimes ignorant, but always well-intentioned. It was so different from Edwardston, and, frankly, most teams he'd been on. He felt a remarkable amount of affection for these idiots, and, in turn, felt less lonely than he had since he'd started playing hockey professionally. But there was another feeling, one he couldn't quite figure out.

He knew perfectly well who to thank for creating a team with a culture like this, but he wasn't sure if anyone else did. If anyone else, except maybe Mike and Alexei, were aware Rupert had, at some point, started doing it *on purpose*.

He thought about that for the rest of their road trip, watching how Rupert handled all the guys on the team—gay, straight, or unknown, accepting, tolerant, or, well—there wasn't anyone Olle would call *in*tolerant, not outwardly, but there were a few who were...taciturn.

He also watched how they all played together, and it struck him how, with those few exceptions, the team played for each other. Olle liked to win, he *always* wanted to win—it was the nature of anyone who fought to become or stay a professional athlete, or they wouldn't have made it this far. But this was different. Olle wanted to win for all the same reasons he ever wanted to win, but now there was something added to that. He wanted to win for Jamie. For Mike and Alexei and Tim and Chris and any other guy who'd been on a team that didn't want them, wouldn't welcome them if they knew the truth, who told them—overtly or implicitly—that there was something wrong with them. Who valued them less because of who they were, not how they played hockey.

And it worked. The Ice Cats were winning. Three out of four on their road trip, and the game the day they got back home. Their already strong season was getting stronger, building momentum. Instead of dragging his ass off the ice, waiting for his scolding, he was running down the tunnel, laughing and jostling with the guys, talking about what they were going to do after the game, complimenting each other on some slick play or another.

And all the while, Rupert and Callum watched over them proudly.

Not unlike how Rupert looked now, sitting at the dining room table with Eleanor in his arms, listening to all he'd missed while they'd been away. Oliver had a new bestie whose parents weren't sure what to make of their daughter trying to develop an English accent, and Christian thought calculus was the devil—Olle didn't disagree—and Callum had found a mechanic, at last, whom he felt he could trust to do an oil change on the minivan.

It was pretty mundane stuff, and Olle wondered what Jamie made of all this. He'd been invited over, again, for dinner. It hadn't even been Olle's idea—Jamie, along with Olle, Mike, and Alexei, had simply been included in the group text from Callum, telling them plenty of food would be waiting after the game, if they'd like to join the family for dinner that night.

Olle had laughed, sitting on the bus next to Jamie when they'd pulled out their simultaneously buzzing phones. Jamie had grinned, then asked, "Do you mind?"

Of course, Olle didn't mind at all. Nor did he miss the not-so-subtle message Callum was sending his way.

Maybe that was why, when they had finished clearing the

table and settled down on the couch to watch some TV, Olle didn't slide his hand into Jamie's under the blankets.

Nope. He did it right on top.

It felt good, and maybe a little scary, like the moment the rollercoaster lets go from its perch on that first high peak. He watched Star Wars Rebels, listening to Oliver's detailed analysis of what each scene meant to the Star Wars universe, and refused to acknowledge the various smirks aimed their way.

It wasn't like everyone here hadn't known, but it still felt big. He thought about how often he'd wanted to hold Jamie's hand over the past few weeks and how many times he had felt like he couldn't.

But he didn't feel that way in this house.

Here he was safe. Jamie was safe. And *that*, he realized, was the funny feeling he had around the team. The one that went beyond affection, and didn't fit solely under friendship.

At its core, particularly with the men who had become their friends, the team made him feel *safe.*

Olle looked over at Rupert and thought he understood a few things better. About the family Rupert had built with Callum and their friends, and about the way he ran the team.

By the time the second episode ended, everyone's long week was catching up with them, and the next day was American Thanksgiving, so no one proposed they try to watch anything else. Oliver mumbled a groggy goodnight and went toward the stairs, Christian staggering after him. Rupert stayed on the couch with Eleanor asleep on his shoulder.

Jamie and Olle stood. Jamie stretched his arms above his head, a huge yawn cracking his jaw, then went limp against Olle's side. "I have to get going. This week has wiped me out."

Olle was concerned when Jamie's eyes fell shut and he leaned all his weight into Olle. He rubbed Jamie's back and looked at Rupert and Callum. "Can Jamie stay here tonight? On the couch, or, umm...with me?" Jamie went still beside him and Olle cursed himself, looking at him quickly. He was wide awake now. "That is, if you want to?"

"Uhh..." Jamie glanced over at Rupert and Callum. "Yes, I would like that." He seemed to be having a hard time deciding if he should smile or not.

Mike and Alexei had no such qualms.

Olle looked back at his landlord-boss-friends and found Rupert looking amused and Callum rolling his eyes. "Just try to remember there are children in the house, please."

And now Olle's face was on fucking *fire,* but that didn't stop him from taking Jamie's hand, towing him into the bedroom, and closing the door with a final goodnight.

Chapter Nine

Jamie could hear the laughter from the living room, knew what they all thought was about to happen, and didn't give a shit that they were absolutely correct.

The moment the door closed, he threw himself at Olle, who caught him, holding him up so he could wrap his legs around Olle's waist and kiss him hard.

"It's okay I asked you to stay, right?" Olle asked when their lips parted.

"I'm here, aren't I?"

"I mean—"

"I know what you mean, and I'm okay with them knowing. I'm okay with any of our families and friends knowing. Not that we have to. We can keep it to the small group who know now, if you want."

"You haven't told your family?" Olle sounded skeptical. He knew how close Jamie was to his sister.

Jamie unwrapped his legs and slid back to his feet, suddenly nervous. He'd been thinking for a while that he and Olle should have a talk about what this is. Where they were going. "They know there's someone," he said.

"But not who?"

Jamie shrugged. "I wasn't sure...I mean, *you and I* hadn't talked about it, so I wasn't sure if I should tell anyone else."

"You can tell them," Olle said.

"Tell them what?" Jamie asked cautiously.

"That I'm your boyfriend."

Jamie grinned. "Oh yeah? And when were you going to tell *me* that?"

Olle drew up short. "Aren't I?"

"No—yes. You are. I mean, I want you to be. I just wasn't

sure if that's how you saw this."

Olle looked almost offended. "This isn't a fling."

"No, of course not," Jamie agreed, laughing and breathless with relief.

"Why is that funny?"

"I don't know," Jamie admitted. "I'm just happy. I was worried…" Jamie bit his lip. Now he knew they were good, he didn't need to go down that road.

"Worried about what?"

"Nothing. It's not important now."

Olle bent down to look directly into Jamie's eyes. It was impossible to look away. "What?"

"That it was just an experiment?"

Olle jerked upright. "No."

Jamie waited for him to say more, but he didn't. "Just…no?"

"I'm not—this isn't…" Olle took a deep breath and let it out slowly. "This may be new, but it's not an experiment. I'm sure about this. About you."

"Okay. Good," Jamie said, his hands sliding around Olle's waist to rest above his hips. "I'm sure about you, too."

Olle kissed him sweetly. "Any more questions?"

"Nope. I'm all out for now."

Olle cupped his hand along Jamie's jaw and dragged his thumb over Jamie's cheekbone. "Good, because it's getting late."

"Oh, yeah? You got big plans?" Jamie teased.

Olle ran a hand over his hip and cupped his ass, his fingers digging in. "Maybe I do."

A hot flush stole over Jamie's entire body. He licked his lips and saw how Olle's eyes tracked the motion. "Tell me what you want," Jamie begged, his brain practically exploding with ideas.

Olle stalked forward, his hands guiding Jamie until he was trapped between Olle's big body and the bed. Jamie squirmed, his thighs pressed against the mattress.

"Can I fuck you?"

Jamie shivered. He was never going to get over how Olle was shy most of the time, but could say something like that while he was staring Jamie in the eyes.

"Yes," Jamie gasped. He wanted that so much, which he'd probably made obvious over the past few weeks.

Olle smiled, his lips still curved when they pressed to Jamie's. His tongue stole into Jamie's mouth.

Jamie melted against him, hanging in his grasp, drowning in Olle. Jamie may have been the one with experience, but Olle was no shrinking violet. He kissed Jamie breathless, then ended it with a nip to his lower lip. He continued to press kisses to Jamie's cheeks, eyelids, and temples.

"How?" Olle murmured as he nibbled his way down Jamie's neck.

"How what?" Jamie groaned, having completely lost the thread of their conversation.

"How do I fuck you?"

Jamie lifted his head and blinked up at Olle. "Um...I mean you—I..." *Did he really not know?* Jamie started at least a half dozen sentences but couldn't string together the words.

Olle burst into laughter. He buried his face in Jamie's neck, snorting with giggles even as he cupped Jamie's ass and wedged his fingers into the crease, right up against his hole. "I understand the mechanics," Olle gasped, still trying to get himself back under control. "I was asking about the *position*."

Jamie slumped with relief, because for a second there he'd thought he was going to have to have the gay birds-and-the-bees talk. Olle captured his mouth and Jamie scrambled backward to get up on the bed. Olle helped, lifting him and moving with him and doing whatever he could so their lips didn't part for more than a few seconds.

Clothes fell away or were tossed. Jamie wasn't sure anymore, and he didn't particularly care. As long as his hands could skim over Olle's wide chest and flat belly, as long as Olle's warm, thick thigh was wedged between his, Jamie knew everything he needed to know.

He ended up on his back on the bed, Olle between his thighs, their cocks pressed together, hard and leaking. Jamie loved being squished into the mattress by his oversized boyfriend—*not getting over being able to call him* that *any time soon*—but Jamie could guess this was the reason Olle had asked about positions. If Olle didn't practically fold himself in half, Jamie was left staring at his chest.

Jamie considered rolling over, getting on his hands and knees or putting himself ass up, but kissing would be difficult and Jamie wanted to be able to see Olle's face. That made the decision easier. In what was becoming his signature move, Jamie heaved his body up off the mattress, pushing Olle to the side until he landed on his back and Jamie could climb up over him.

Olle lay back, arms spread, smile lethal.

Jamie nudged at his ribs, making Olle squirm up the bed until he was propped against the pillows and the headboard. He bent his knees, and Jamie settled into his lap. They groaned when Jamie canted his hips and their cocks rolled together.

"Like this?" Jamie said, running his hands up Olle's chest.

Olle grabbed a couple more pillows, propped his shoulders higher, and curled his palm around the back of Jamie's neck to pull him in for a long kiss. "Yes," he murmured when they came up for air. "This is perfect."

He skimmed his thumb over Jamie's cheekbone, and ran a hand all the way down Jamie's back, tucking his fingertips into the crease of Jamie's ass and making him wriggle.

Then he had a sudden, terrible, thought. "Do you have lube? And condoms?"

A slow smile grew on Olle's face. "*Now* you think of this?"

Jamie poked Olle in the chest. "To be fair, I came over for dinner. I never in my wildest dreams thought we'd get Dad and Dad's blessing for a sleepover."

Olle laughed, stretching his arm out to reach his bedside table and pulling the drawer open. Jamie dove for the contents as soon as he saw what was inside.

Settled back onto Olle's lap, he swiveled his hips in a dirty grind and watched pleasure race over Olle's face. He kept at it as he popped open the cap to the lube and squirted some onto his fingers.

Olle's stopped him with a hand wrapped around his wrist. "What are you doing?"

Maybe he needed to do that birds-and-the-bees thing after all. "Um...I have to, you know, prepare myself for..."

He trailed off when Olle shook his head, clearly amused, and maybe just a little exasperated, before tugging the bottle of lube from Jamie's hand.

Jamie sat there with lube trickling down his fingers until Olle guided his hand down.

"You use that here," he said, pressing Jamie's hand to his dick and making him hiss. "And I'll handle this," he said, running a fingertip over Jamie's hole.

Jamie shuddered.

"If that's okay?" Olle asked, circling his fingertip again.

Jamie nodded, no longer able to speak. He ran a slick hand up his shaft and what little blood was left in his brain went straight to his cock.

Olle could watch Jamie's face all night. He could get off just on the way Jamie's eyes fluttered shut and he chewed on his lips, the wriggle of his hips as he slid his slick hand up and down his cock. Then Olle's.

He almost fumbled the lube, but managed to save it at the last second and spare himself another laughing fit when Jamie became worried, again, that Olle didn't know how two men could have sex together.

Olle knew. In fact, he was accumulating a list in his head of all the ways he wanted to have sex with Jamie. It was not a short list, either.

He slicked his fingers and tapped at Jamie's tight hole, rubbing the lubricant around the skin and letting Jamie get used to the growing pressure. Jamie hummed happily.

"Is there anything I should know?" Olle asked as he pushed a little harder, the tip of his middle finger dipping between the tightly furled muscles before retreating.

Jamie gasped. "Like what?"

"I don't know. I usually go fast, but I like it to burn a little and you might not."

Jamie's eyes snapped open. "I thought you never—"

"I like fingering myself," Olle said, his cheeks getting warm, but his eyes steady on Jamie's. He really needed to disabuse him of this idea that he was *that* inexperienced.

"You do?"

"Yes. Next time it can be you fucking me. If you want."

Jamie's face went from pink to red, but Olle didn't think it was embarrassment. No, based on the way Jamie was practically strangling his own cock, he wasn't opposed to the idea at all.

"Jesus, you're going to kill me," Jamie muttered.

Olle took that as the perfect time to slip his middle finger into Jamie's ass.

Jamie's head fell back on his neck and he groaned. "*Olle.*"

Arousal throbbed in Olle, barely leaving him with the coordination to kiss Jamie and cut off whatever else he might say before they either got kicked out or the entire household started applauding.

Jamie gripped Olle's hair in a tight fist and kissed him back, his hips rolling slowly as he fucked himself on Olle's finger. Olle held his hand steady and gave Jamie the resistance he needed, letting Jamie take control while Olle kissed him long and as hard.

When he pulled his lips away, he pressed his forehead to Jamie's and whispered, "You have to be quiet."

Jamie never stopped moving, still fucking himself with Olle's dick caught between them. "Okay," he murmured.

Olle was desperate to move things along, his cock leaking onto his belly, his balls drawn up tight. He teased the tip of his index finger around Jamie's rim, feeling how the muscle gave.

Jamie stuttered to a stop, his mouth dropping open when Olle pressed the second finger inside.

"Good?"

Jamie nodded, face flushed and eyes almost feverishly bright. Olle was trying not to look any one place too long or think about how tight and hot Jamie was inside.

They both groaned when Jamie started moving again. Olle met his thrusts this time, scissoring his fingers gently. Jamie liked that, nodding even more vigorously but staying silent as he picked up his pace and Olle stretched him further. Olle swore that the next time they did this, it would be somewhere they could yell their fucking heads off if they wanted.

Jamie kept rocking, and Olle kept stretching him open, keeping a careful eye on Jamie's face for signs of pain or discomfort. Jamie seemed lost to whatever he was feeling, his eyes on Olle but his gaze vague, his blinks slow.

His hands, pressed to Olle's chest above his heart, began to tremble.

Olle added more lube, pushing it into Jamie until his fingers moved with almost no resistance. When Jamie's eyebrows drew down, when the pinch of his teeth on his poor, abused lower lip got white around the edges, Olle slid the third finger in.

He was ready to kiss Jamie if he let out a shout. To reverse course if he looked freaked out or uncomfortable. Olle knew how much the third finger could be. He loved it, but not everyone was like him.

Jamie surprised him by seeming to come back into himself, his eyes narrowed and focused, his hand suddenly patting across the mattress beside them. He made a triumphant noise and held a condom aloft, then ripped the foil open with his teeth. Olle bit his cheek hard, the pain a necessary distraction as Jamie made quick work of rolling the latex down Olle's shaft.

It was a miracle Olle didn't blow on the spot.

Jamie curled his hand around Olle's cock. "I'm ready," he said, breathless, knee walking higher and keeping his hold on Olle.

Olle eased his fingers out of Jamie's ass. "What do you want me to do?"

Jamie smiled, his tongue caught between his teeth as he settled above Olle. "Hold still."

Olle nodded, his breath stuttering when the head of his cock pressed against Jamie's hole. Olle had the somewhat hysterical thought that there was no way he was going to fit, that bodies just couldn't work this way.

He kept that to himself rather than prove Jamie's suspicions about how naïve he was. He ran his hands up and down Jamie's trembling thighs, cupping his ass to support some of his weight and spreading him open in the process.

"Yes," Jamie hissed, putting more weight into Olle's hands. Jamie's body gave in to the pressure. Olle swore to fucking god he could feel every single millimeter Jamie stretched open.

Olle lay panting, the pressure on his cock so intense, so tight, it almost hurt. He worried this *was* hurting Jamie and was about to tell Jamie to stop, to suggest they go back to fingering and maybe come that way, when the head of his cock popped past Jamie's rim and the muscles clamped around him.

"Oh my fucking god—mmph—"

Jamie's mouth cut off his exclamation, but *holy shit*, how was Olle supposed to keep his shit together when Jamie was like a vice around him? Incredible heat and pressure concentrated right on the head of his cock made him want to scream with pleasure.

Olle didn't know what the hell he'd been expecting, but it hadn't been anything this overwhelming. He eased back from Jamie's kiss, murmuring soft apologies for being too loud. For stretching Jamie open this far. His fingers traced the stretched skin around his shaft, amazed.

Jamie laughed, breathlessly, and Olle stared up at his beautiful face. He couldn't stop touching where his cock disappeared into Jamie's body. He had a sudden, brilliant flash of what it would be like to have Jamie spearing into his body this way.

"Next time I want you to fuck me," he whispered hoarsely.

Jamie's laughter died with a whimper. "Let's finish this first, okay?" he said, then sank further down Olle's shaft.

Olle's head spun, his thighs trembling from holding still so long. Jamie took another moment to adjust before taking up a slow rhythm that worked Olle's cock deeper with each roll of Jamie's hips.

Olle ran his hands over Jamie's back, his ass and his thighs, occasionally dipping between their bodies, unable to resist tracing the place they were joined. Every time he sank farther into Jamie, a little more of his control slipped from his grasp.

He didn't move, though. He'd said he wouldn't move.

Jamie pressed his palms to Olle's chest, using his arms as leverage as he lifted himself up. Then he let his weight and gravity do the work as he slid down to press fully into Olle's lap. Sweat trickled down Olle's face, down the back of his neck. He wanted to move so badly he shook.

Jamie's eyes fluttered shut and that was almost Olle's undoing. He watched avidly as Jamie shifted minutely, here and there, settling more fully onto Olle's cock. His face twitched, flushed with pleasure and never more gorgeous.

"Fuck, Olle," he murmured. "You feel amazing."

Olle nodded. "So...so do you."

Jamie opened his eyes and frowned. "Are you okay?"

Olle tried to smile, but it wobbled. "I really want to move," he confessed.

Jamie looked sympathetic but didn't take back his request for Olle to hold still. Instead, he shifted more of his weight to his arms to slowly lift himself off Olle, and holy hell, Olle tried not to squirm, but the drag of Jamie's tight rim up his cock was fucking exquisite, his quick descent mind-blowing.

Olle clapped a hand over his mouth, not trusting himself. His skin prickled with sweat, his heels digging into the bed to hold them steady, to try to ground himself.

Jamie bit his lip, his face a mask of concentration as he

fucked himself on Olle's cock again. And again. Soon he was landing in Olle's lap with a solid thump and a soft cry, the mattress bouncing beneath them as Olle's cock went deep into the tight clench of Jamie's ass. Jamie picked up speed and pleasure fired through Olle's body, his spine arching as Jamie took him to the edge of reason.

"*Now.* Now you can move. *Please,*" Jamie said, a quiet and heartfelt plea.

Olle snapped his hips up, meeting Jamie's ass with a firm smack before they landed on the bed together. Olle couldn't stop the noise that came up out of his chest. His heart. Jamie's hand gripped Olle's shoulder, so tight there would be bruises in the morning, but that and Olle's hand on his hip kept Jamie stable as he and Olle rocked against one another, their motions frantic. It was less of a graceful dance and more of a desperate wrestling match, but they'd get better at this. They'd practice *all the time* if Olle had anything to say about it. They were professional athletes, by god. They would master the hell out of this.

Olle started to lose what little rhythm he had, his orgasm clawing at him. He almost slipped out of Jamie, his coordination blown, before thrusting back in at a different angle.

Jamie let out a frantic, high-pitched noise, his hips canting like he was chasing Olle's cock, chasing the sensation. Olle stayed still, shaking and furiously trying to stave off his orgasm, until Jamie made the noise again, having found the angle he wanted. Needed.

Now it was Jamie who held still, while Olle thrust into him, hard and fast, and Jamie stared at him with wide, sightless eyes.

Olle could feel the last tether of his control slipping from his grasp. He curled his hand around Jamie's cock, dragging his fist up the length, squeezing tight. Jamie screwed his eyes shut, his nails piercing Olle's shoulder as he nodded. Olle thought he could almost see the climax swelling inside Jamie. He was fucking gorgeous like this—sheened with sweat as he shuddered and keened, teetering on the edge.

From one thrust to the next, Olle lost the battle to hold back his own orgasm, the dam breaking and letting it crash over him. His hips slammed up into Jamie and Jamie rode him back down onto the bed, absolutely coming apart in his arms. In his lap. He pressed his face to Olle's, his breath gusting across Olle's lips as he squeezed around Olle's cock like a vise, a hot splash of his cum spattering across Olle's abs and dripping into his navel.

Olle wrapped his arms around Jamie, holding him close, breathing in his scent and memorizing every sound. Every sensation. Jamie's soft skin. The heat pouring off his body. The scratch of his stubble. The width of his shoulders.

But most of all, Olle tried to capture the feeling in his chest. The hot, tight, sweet ache that had been growing beneath his ribs for weeks had bloomed into something big. So big it was scary, but still something Olle wanted more than anything.

Chapter Ten

Olle woke up early to the sounds of pots and pans being slung around the kitchen. He knew Alexei and Callum were responsible, and he could tell they were trying to keep it down, but they were hosting Thanksgiving dinner for their friends and most of the team tonight, so there was a ton of cooking to be done.

Olle tried to go back to sleep, pulling Jamie in tight against his chest and enjoying his warmth, smiling as he remembered the times one of them had woken up in the night and immediately crawled back into the arms of the other. Jamie had gotten up a few hours ago to go to the bathroom. When he'd come back, he'd buried his face in Olle's chest and promptly begun snoring again.

Olle liked it. A lot. So much so, he was considering asking Jamie if he wanted to look for an apartment together. There was no rush, of course, since they were able to stay where they were for the rest of the season, and Olle was fairly confident both sets of doting billet parents would be cool with one or the other of them spending the night. But the privacy, the shared space, would be nice.

Less like dating and more like having a partner.

The question was if Jamie was ready for that. Again, there was no hurry, Olle reminded himself. It hadn't been two months since they'd come to Moncton, and this season wasn't even halfway over, so they had lots of time before they should worry about next season and where to live.

Olle knew what he felt, what he wanted, but he wouldn't rush Jamie. He *did* want to tell Jamie how he felt, but he wasn't sure if Jamie was ready for that, either.

Olle sighed. His brain was firing too fast for him to get back to sleep, and the noise from the rest of the house was going to steadily increase. It was only a matter of time before his conscience got the best of him and he would go help.

In the meantime, he wanted to start the day off right.

He wasn't surprised when Jamie slept through Olle pulling his arm out from under his head and replacing it with a pillow. And he could see how, after Jamie had played his heart out for the last series of games, he might not wake up when Olle slithered under the sheets. But Olle was starting to worry when he had most of Jamie's hardening cock in his mouth and still nothing.

Then a hand clenched tight into his hair.

"Jesus Christ," Jamie gasped a moment before he sat up and the covers were thrown off Olle's head.

Olle didn't release Jamie's cock from his lips, so it wasn't like he could respond. He did smile, as best he could, which made Jamie groan again, louder.

All sound stopped in the kitchen for the span of one heartbeat, then resumed, louder than before.

Jamie's eyes widened with alarm. Olle sucked harder, his cheeks hollowing as he dragged his lips up Jamie's fully hard shaft.

Jamie's mouth dropped open, his lips forming an 'O' in an excellent approximation of Olle's. Olle was a little concerned about Jamie making a loud noise, but so was Jamie, apparently, because he flopped back down onto the bed and buried his face beneath a pillow he held in place with his entire arm.

Olle released Jamie's cock with an obscene pop, chuckling as he licked down the shaft and buried his nose in the coarse hair at the base. He scratched the stubble on his chin along Jamie's inner thighs and Jamie spread them, his knees coming up until his feet left the bed.

A shudder of desire worked its way down Olle's spine, blood surging into his cock.

He ducked his head to suck and lick Jamie's sac, relishing the whimpers leaking out from beneath the pillow as he tried different things. He sucked one ball into his mouth, curling his tongue around it, and immediately knew he'd found a winner.

Jamie's legs twitched, one heel planting on the ball of Olle's shoulder as Jamie spread his huge, gorgeous thighs open further in invitation.

Olle licked and sucked, kissed and nibbled everything he could reach while Jamie made increasingly desperate noises into the pillow. His neglected cock leaked onto his belly, the head an angry red, the shaft riddled with veins. Olle almost felt sorry, but he was enjoying his explorations too much to stop. Not until he had tasted every inch of Jamie—or Jamie asked him to stop.

When Olle slid his tongue along the seam of skin behind Jamie's balls, rubbing and teasing, Jamie's foot dug into Olle's shoulder and his ass lifted off the mattress.

Olle swiped the broad flat of his tongue over Jamie's hole, his hands clamping around Jamie's hips and holding him up when he shuddered and his foot slipped down Olle's back. The faint taste of lube wasn't great, but Olle licked again, groaning when he realized that Jamie's rim was still a little swollen.

God, *he'd* done that.

Olle dove in, giving Jamie his enthusiastic attention until Jamie's balls pulled up tight and he clamped a hand around the base of his cock. Then Olle backed off, nosing along the crease between Jamie's thigh and ass while sucking one of his own fingers into his mouth. He eased Jamie back onto the bed, letting him settle before sliding his cock back into his mouth and pushing his slick finger into Jamie's ass.

Jamie thrashed, his chest heaving as Olle thrust his finger gently and sucked Jamie's cock as deep as he dared.

Jamie clamped the pillow over his face with both arms, arched his back clear off the bed, and came with a muffled cry.

Olle swallowed quickly, drawing out Jamie's orgasm until he shivered. Olle let Jamie's cock slip from his lips and lay panting between Jamie's splayed thighs, sweaty and hot and so fucking turned on. He ground his hips into the mattress while he caught his breath, dizzily trying to figure out if coming on Jamie when he was semi-incoherent would be rude.

A pillow sailed over Olle's head, then Jamie's fingers

threaded into his hair and tugged, towing Olle up his body and into a long, filthy kiss. Jamie hummed at the taste of his own come on Olle's tongue and pushed at Olle's chest until he fell back against the cool footboard.

Olle stared up at Jamie as he climbed between Olle's legs, Olle's cock sliding along Jamie's warm skin, leaking and painfully hard.

The familiar snick of a cap sent a shiver down Olle's spine.

Jamie pressed a kiss behind Olle's ear. "You said you like it to burn a little, right?" A cool, slick finger slid from behind Olle's tight sac to swirl over his hole.

He nodded, words failing him.

Jamie moved back far enough to see Olle's face, a smile flashing at whatever he saw before he caught Olle's lower lip between his teeth and slid two fingers into his ass.

Olle went off like a fucking rocket.

Ten minutes later, Jamie lay sprawled across Olle's chest, his chin propped on his folded hands, listening to him talk about what he was going to ship home to his parents for Christmas.

A gentle knock on the door made them freeze.

"If you two are...*ahem*...awake now," Callum began, lifting his voice to be heard over the snickering from several other people on the other side of the door, "I could use Olle's help with the extra tables in storage."

"Do you want me to shower first?" Olle asked.

"How is that even a question?" Rupert cried. Jamie didn't think he was asking Olle.

"Give me ten minutes!" Olle called, laughing.

Jamie was about to roll off him but Olle cupped his hand around the back of his head and drew him into a kiss. They burned one whole minute before Jamie pulled away and Olle sighed with disappointment.

Jamie slid to the side and curled up with his head on the pillows. "You go shower, and I'll dash home to clean up and change."

"Do you want to spend the night again?"

Jamie caught his lip between his teeth. "Do you think it would be okay?"

"I'll ask the Dads and text you, okay? If that's a yes."

"Yes. Yes, it's definitely a yes," Jamie promised.

"Good," Olle said, climbing from the bed. He smiled down at Jamie, his long hair hanging half in his face. He was so beautiful it made Jamie's chest ache.

Olle bent down and kissed Jamie's cheek. "I love you."

Jamie stared at Olle's magnificent ass as he wandered into the bathroom like he hadn't just dropped a bomb on Jamie. The door clicked closed, spurring Jamie to leap from the bed, torn between jumping into the shower with Olle and running home to pack a bag and come back as soon as possible. He stuck with the plan, but only because there was an entire household outside this room and he was certain Olle would never meet his ten minute commitment if Jamie went into that bathroom.

The distance from the bedroom to the front door was the closest Jamie had ever come to doing a walk of shame—except he felt absolutely *no* shame at all. He couldn't wipe the grin off his face, though he did blush furiously at his audience's obvious delight and amusement. Thank god the children were still downstairs.

When he got back to the apartment, Chris and Tim were curled up together on the couch, watching a cooking show and bickering about whether or not Tim should iron Chris's shirt for the party.

"Yes, you should," Jamie said as he jogged past them. "It's your bosses' party."

"Have a nice night?" Chris shouted down the hall as Jamie ducked into his room.

When Jamie reappeared with a small duffel and darted to the laundry closet, Tim hooted with laughter. "I guess you did."

"I definitely did," Jamie agreed, the stupid grin back on his face as he shoved things into the bag. He was probably packing too much, but there was the party, and they didn't have a game for two days, so while he wasn't sure if he should stay that long, he wanted to have stuff in case.

Chris wandered down the hall and leaned against the dryer. "Hey."

"Hey," Jamie said back, flashing him a smile before turning for his room again.

Chris trailed in his wake. "You moving out?" he asked curiously as Jamie grabbed the toiletries kit he kept packed for road trips.

Jamie stopped what he was doing and turned to his friend. "What? No."

Chris arched an eyebrow.

"I don't want to move out," Jamie said.

"Yet," Chris added.

"Yet," Jamie agreed, sharing a smile with Chris. He opened his mouth, and closed it again.

Chris nudged his arm. "What?"

"Would it be okay with you guys if Olle spent the night sometimes?"

"Sure," Chris said easily. "But if he's going to move in, he has to pay rent."

"No. I don't think—not yet. Not in the middle of the season. But maybe he and I will look at places for next season."

"Oh, yeah?"

Jamie grinned. "Yes. I mean, I have to talk to him about it, but..."

Chris nodded. "Good for you."

Jamie tackle-hugged Chris and held on tight. "Thank you."

"For what?"

"Getting me here. With Olle."

"I had almost nothing to do with you, and definitely can't take responsibility for Olle. Rupert wanted you from the minute I mentioned you needed a move."

"God, I'm so lucky he needed a winger."

"No, dude. Haven't you figured it out yet?"

Jamie let go and stepped back. "What?"

"I mean, yes, you're lucky, but he's doing it on purpose. Building a—okay, I don't want to say a gay team, because obviously that's not what it is, or all it is, and we have tons of straight guys still, but yeah, I told him what happened and he went after you like a dog with a bone."

"Because I'm gay?"

"I mean, *and* because you're a great winger, but a great winger who was outed and struggling. You needed help. And he took Olle because he figured out Olle was protecting you on the ice, taking all those insane penalties. Rupert didn't know if Olle was gay or straight. He just knew he'd fit here with us."

"For real?"

"Yes." Chris laughed, sounding as incredulous as Jamie felt. "It's crazy."

"We're winning," Jamie said, almost defensively, not that Chris needed to hear it.

"We are. And we will. Rupert told me his theory is that teams are great when they play for each other. When they have a shared purpose. I think Vegas convinced him of it once and for all. The right mix of talent still matters, but to win and push and really *want it*, you have to have a reason. He believes we can win it all if we have that."

"We do. Have that," Jamie said, realization setting in.

"And we're winning," Chris agreed with a nod.

"Holy shit," Jamie whispered.

Chris smirked knowingly and left him to his packing.

By the time Jamie was showered and dressed and had his bag by the door, he was *itching* to get going. Olle had texted to say he could spend the night again and Jamie wanted to see his bag on the floor next to Olle's travel bags. His stuff mixed with Olle's in the bathroom.

God, he had it so bad.

The second he could leave and not show up at the party absurdly early, he was out the door like a shot. He was across town, parked, and to Rupert and Callum's door before panic set in. *Shit*, how was he going to explain bringing an overnight bag to Thanksgiving dinner?

Callum opened the door and smirked. "Jamie, so nice to see you again."

Jamie shook Callum's hand and smiled weakly, trying to figure out a graceful way to go back down to his car.

"Here, let me take your coat," Callum said smoothly. "We're stacking them on the bed in the guest room," he explained, sliding the duffle bag from Jamie's shoulder to his own and folding Jamie's coat over his arm.

The guy was slick. Jamie smiled up at him gratefully. "Thank you so much for inviting me." He wasn't just talking about the party.

"I'm trying to decide at what point I should start charging rent."

"I'm getting that talk a lot today."

Callum chuckled and turned for Olle's room. Jamie went to the kitchen to ask if Alexei needed help and was waved off, left feeling useless until Rupert asked him to answer the door.

Jamie took on welcoming duty for a while, taking turns ferrying coats to Olle's room, all the while making lingering eye contact with his boyfriend—*still loving that*—while he manned the makeshift bar at one corner of the kitchen counter. The apartment filled with a good portion of the team, and two dozen other people Jamie had never met before. He tried to remember all their names, but it was a lost cause. Rupert and Callum were active members of the community, and there were people from all walks of life, from as far as Nova Scotia, Boston, and Montreal.

The conversation went from a din to a dull roar as the food was served and some of the guests enjoyed their second or third drink. Jamie gravitated toward Olle more and more, pleased when Olle was shooed away from the bar and encouraged to mingle.

Jamie chuckled at the face Olle made at the idea of mingling, guiding him toward a group of their friends to spare him the torture. Jamie listened with one ear as the guys razzed Olle's man-bun and Chris's unusually tidy shirt, and watched the party unfold.

Olle bumped his shoulder after a while, his voice low. "You okay?"

"Yeah. I'm fine. I was just thinking how lucky we are to have been traded here."

Olle smiled. "Yes."

Jamie watched Callum and Alexei bicker affectionately over the stove, clearly giving each other shit about something. Rupert wandered close enough to the kitchen to hear what they were saying, rolled his eyes, and walked away.

Jamie glanced at Olle and found he was watching Rupert as he moved around the room. "I'm not sure if it's luck, though," Olle observed.

"No. Maybe not." Jamie agreed, stepping aside to let Oliver and his bestie rush by. When he moved back to Olle, he leaned in closer and brushed their hands together. "But I feel lucky. Luckier than I deserve, to have this team. And you," he said.

Olle turned to him. "Yeah?"

"Yeah. If you hadn't walked away this morning, I would have had a chance to tell you."

"Tell me what?"

"That I love you."

A smile lit up Olle's face. Jamie thought anyone who saw him would be able to tell what was going on between them. He almost warned Olle, suggested he tone it down, but Olle shocked him by stepping closer and taking his hand. Then the other, his smile never dimming, his gaze never leaving Jamie's face.

The conversations around them trailed off, their friends and teammates going silent. The whole party could have gone silent, for all Jamie knew. His entire world had narrowed down to Olle.

"This okay?" Olle asked, cheeks pink but voice steady.

"Yes. *Yes.* Are *you* sure?"

"I am," Olle said. "I'm sure about you, and I'm sure about us, and I'm sure about this." He cupped Jamie's face in his hands and kissed him softly, sweetly, on the lips.

Jamie's heart was full to bursting with joy, the future full of promise and hockey and *love.*

Then he and Olle were tackled by a dozen of the most ridiculous hockey players on earth, and that was pretty perfect, too.

About the Author

Samantha Wayland has three great loves in life; her family, writing books, and hockey. She is often found apologizing to the first for how much time and attention is taken up by the latter two, but they forgive her because they are awesome and she clearly doesn't deserve them.

Sam lives with her family—of both the two and four-legged variety—outside of Boston. She is a wicked passionate New Englander (born and raised) who has been known to wax rhapsodic about the Maine Coast, the mountains of New Hampshire and Vermont, and the sensible way in which her local brethren don't see a need for directional signals (blinkahs!). When she's not locked away in her home office, she can generally be found tucked in the corner of the local Thai place with other socially-starved authors and an adult beverage.

Her favorite things include mango martinis, tiny Chihuahuas with big attitude problems, and the Oxford comma.

Sam loves to hear from readers. Email her at samantha@samanthawayland.com or find her on Facebook, Twitter (@samwayland), and Instagram (SamWayRomance).